Nicky Fifth Explores

New Jersey's
Great Outdoors

by Lisa Funari Willever

Franklin Mason Press
Trenton, New Jersey

*To Governor Brendan T. Byrne, for your dedication to
New Jersey's future, your example to our youngest citizens,
and your wisdom regarding our Great Outdoors.*

*Special thanks to Anne Salvatore, Wanda Swanson, Dawn
Hiltner, Jennifer Wahner, Iris Hutchinson, Allyssa Barnes,
Lauren Lambiase, Marcia Jacobs, Karen Funari, Linda Funari,
and Nancy Byrne...all amazing women.*

Franklin Mason Press ISBN 978-0-9857218-1-7
Library of Congress Control Number: 2013948193

Editorial and Production Staff: Jennifer Wahner, Shoshana
Hurwitz, Marcia Jacobs, Iris Hutchinson, Allyssa Barnes, Mary
Sullivan, and Linda Funari.

Contents

The Nicky Fifth Series

written by
Award-winning author Lisa Funari Willever,
Winner of the 2009 Benjamin Franklin Award

A Letter from the Author

Dear Readers,

While Nicky Fifth and T-Bone have been enjoying many Garden State Adventures, my readers have had the opportunity to follow along in the story and in real life. Using *real New Jersey* locations as the setting has introduced a new generation to our amazing state.

In book seven, *Vote For T-Bone*, readers learned about New Jersey government, civics, and politics. This information is necessary to become informed and involved in the decisions that affect everyone.

Now, Nicky and T-Bone have Mission NJGO to save New Jersey's Great Outdoors. As the most densely populated state, we are fortunate to have such a diverse landscape. We have a responsibility to *protect and enjoy* these wonderful places. Education is the first step; know what you're protecting and why it needs protection.

But there's more; the best way to really protect our natural resources is to visit them. You see, when people stop visiting places like state parks and forests, lawmakers stop spending money on them. Without strong attendance and steady funding, these sites cannot survive. I invite you to join me, along with Nicky Fifth, T-Bone, and Wanda, as we begin MISSION: SAVING NJGO.

Not only will you learn about more amazing NJ destinations and their history, you'll also learn about the contributions of people like Governor Brendan T. Byrne. Visit the places Nicky, T-Bone, and Wanda visit and learn about the issues facing our Great Outdoors.

And be sure to check out our Nicky Fifth contests for opportunities to write, share New Jersey destinations, and support great causes. This book features the winners of our special contests, so I urge you to keep reading after the story ends to learn about these talented students and to enjoy their work.

Explore New Jersey, enjoy New Jersey!

Lisa Funari Willever

Chapter One

"Good morning," said T-Bone with his typical, goofy smile. "I *cannot* wait for today."

"Then you're in luck," I laughed. "Today is here."

"No, I mean, I can't wait to get to school and finally start my official presidency," he explained.

"You mean your *co-presidency*," I corrected, reminding him that he wasn't the only class president.

Thanks to some goofy-back-room-closed-door-strawberry-shampoo-induced decision, he was suddenly the co-president with a girl named Wanda. I never got the whole story, but it was *very suspicious*. I knew we had the lead going into the election. I also knew T-Bone seemed to have a major crush on his opponent; an opponent who purposely washed her hair with strawberry shampoo. Things just didn't add up. He would never admit it, but I believed the whole co-presidency idea was 100% Wanda's idea. Furthermore, I believed she convinced my friend that it was actually *his idea*.

"So where do you think our oval offices will be?" he asked.

"Excuse me?" I said. "Did you just ask me where your oval offices would be?"

"You know, our presidential offices," he repeated. "We're both student council president, so I assume we'll each have an office. I just hope my office is in the main hallway; near Wanda, you know, so we can talk politics."

"I'm sure it's in the hall," I said, "and I bet it's really cozy."

"Cozy sounds small, Nick," he replied with a furrowed brow. "Don't you watch those house-flipping shows?"

"No," I said. "I guess that depends on what you consider small. I'm thinking twelve inches wide by six feet tall."

"That's not very big," he thought out loud. "What about a window?"

"Yeah, I'm sure you'll have vents instead of windows."

"Wait a minute!" he demanded. "If I didn't know better, I would think you're describing a locker."

"I know," I laughed. "You thought you'd get an office?"

"Of course," he insisted. "I'm an elected official."

"Correction, you are *half of an elected official*," I said. "Remember our hard-fought campaign was reduced to some kind of preschool tie where everyone's a winner?"

"You know, you don't wear bitter well," he shook his head. "Anyway, why does our sharing the presidency bother you so much? Two heads are better than one, right?"

"I'm not bitter," I replied, "I'm a realist. How's it gonna work if you have equal power, but disagree, then what?"

"We'll discuss it like civilized people and compromise."

"And what if you each feel very strongly about an issue, but neither one is willing to budge, then what?"

"Nick, Nick, you worry too much," he insisted. "I doubt that there's any issue that will cause Wanda and I to disagree. *How could anything possibly go wrong?*"

I remembered news clips of other countries and elected officials throwing food at one another, having major brawls. I hoped T-Bone knew what he was talking about.

"So where should we go next?" I asked, reminding him that we were still junior ambassadors of New Jersey and there was more to think about than just student council.

"That's a good question," he nodded. "Let me check with Wanda and get back to you."

"Check with who, what, who do you, what are you talking about?" I asked. He couldn't seriously think Wanda would help us decide where to go next, could he?

"I think we should have my co-president join us," he said.

"Join us as what?" I asked. "*We're the co-ambassadors*!"

"I just thought she might have good ideas," he explained.

"So you want her to plan the trips with us?" I asked.

"Plan *and go on*," he nodded.

"No," I said, shaking my head.

"What?" he asked.

"No," I repeated. "You and Wanda are co-presidents, but she's *not* the third junior ambassador. This is a two-person gig and *we're* the two people. What if I wanted to help make all of the decisions for student council with you?"

"That would be awful," he agreed.

"Exactly," I said. "It wouldn't be right."

"Not that," he said. "It's 'cause you haven't been elected."

"Very funny," I smirked, "but you can't seriously think Wanda will be planning our day trips, do you?"

"Why not?" he asked. "She lives in New Jersey and she's smart and her... *never mind*."

"Her what?" I asked. "What were you about to say?"

"Nothing," he mumbled, refusing to make eye contact.

"You were gonna say her hair smells like strawberries!"

"No, I was gonna say that, um, her, uh, I mean, she has..."

"Admit it, you were gonna say that her hair smells like strawberries," I insisted. "Just admit it."

"Fine, I admit it," he began, "her hair doesn't just smell like strawberries, it's a different fruit every day. I never know what it will be. One day it's strawberry, then the next day it's grape, and then when you least expect it, *boom*, mandarin orange! I don't know how she does it."

"Yeah, that's a fascinating story," I said with an eye roll. "So her hair smells like produce, *big deal*. That doesn't make her an *almost Official Ambassador of New Jersey.*"

"Nick, she's really nice and really smart," he persisted, "and I know if you give her a chance, you'll like her."

"I don't dislike her," I said, "I don't even really know her; I just like things the way they are."

"Perfect!" he exclaimed, not hearing a word I said. "So

you'll give her a shot? You won't regret this. *Trust me.*"

The last time I trusted T-Bone, I was holding my brother, Timmy, by the ankles and shoving him into a garbage can to look for stickers to earn an anniversary gift for my parents. I didn't have a good feeling about Wanda, but there was no changing T-Bone's mind. I wondered if Wanda loved him as much as he obviously loved her. If she did, these day trips would be absolutely miserable. I'd have to watch them smile at each other all day, laughing at non-funny jokes and sharing snacks. This could, quite possibly, be the worst news I had received in a long time.

"Nick, Nick, snap out of it," he said, waving his hands in front of my face. "The bus is here! Don't worry, Wanda won't be on it because co-presidents can't ride on the same bus. You know, like the president and vice-president of the United States. *It's probably a federal law.*"

"Yeah," I said, "I'm sure it has nothing to do with where she lives. You know her street isn't on our route, right?"

"Exactly," he said. "That's because we're co-presidents."

He really thought there was a law about student council presidents riding together. It was absurd, but it could be good. If they couldn't ride on the same bus together, they certainly couldn't ride in the same car together. That meant she couldn't tag along. Thank you, T-Bone, I thought to myself; in one minute he created and solved a problem. *Thanks, buddy.*

Chapter Two

By the time lunch rolled around, I was starving. For the past two years, I ate lunch at 10:30 in the morning. It was so early they should have called it brunch. Now, we ate at 12:15 and it felt like midnight. T-Bone sat at his usual seat with his usual lunch; basically everything his mom had handy. And, even with an enormous sandwich, assorted fruits, chopped vegetables, and two snacks, he still had time to talk to twenty people each day.

But today was different; he didn't try to talk to twenty people. Today, he had one person on his mind. *Today he invited Wanda to sit at our table.*

"Hey, Wanda! Wanda! Over here, Wanda! Hey, Madame President!" he yelled. "Do you wanna eat at our table?"

"What?" she asked as she slowly turned around. "And why are you calling me *Madame President*?"

"Because it would be rude to call you Mister President," he shrugged. "Anyway, I was wondering if you wanted to have lunch with me; *I mean, us.*"

"Just because we're co-presidents doesn't mean we have to eat together," she said. "Unless there's an urgent issue."

That should do it, I thought. There were no urgent issues. Perfect. No issues meant no Wanda.

"Actually, Nicky and I have something we'd both like to discuss with you," he blurted out. "Oh, and it's urgent."

"We do?" I asked.

"Sure, we do," he said, giving me the *if you're really my friend, you'll go along with this* look. His eyes were filled with desperation. As he bit his lower lip, a bead of sweat ran down his forehead and right into his eye.

"No, we don't," I replied, determined to keep Wanda at another table. It was for his own good.

"Yes, we do," he insisted, squinting so hard he reminded me of my mom when we had company. "Remember, that thing we needed to discuss with Wanda? That thing? You know what I'm talking about. That thing!"

"Sorry, there's no *thing*," I tormented him. "It was nice seeing you, Wanda. I'll call you if a *thing* comes up."

Just as she was about to walk away, and in a moment of sheer desperation, T-Bone blurted out those words I'll never forget. "Wanda, we wanted to know if you'd like to help us with our Official Junior Ambassador jobs."

"What?" Wanda and I both asked at the same time.

"Remember, Nick?" he asked, with his sweaty eyes.

"That's actually an interesting idea," she mumbled as she thought out loud. "I do respect what you do and I'd love to help my state. But then there's my honors classes and student council. That would be a lot on my plate."

"Yeah, that's true; you don't want to put too much on your plate. With honors and student council, you probably wouldn't have time for New Jersey. That's too bad," I said, realizing I had to put this fire out fast. "But don't worry, Wanda, we'll take care of New Jersey."

"On the other hand," T-Bone continued, "you love New Jersey and you know if you're not part of the solution, your part of the problem. Joining us as ambassadors is like you're patriotic New Jersey duty."

"*Patriotic New Jersey duty?*" I asked, wondering if there was any way to make him stop talking. "*Joining us?*"

"Well," she started, "I definitely have my hands full…"

"Full hands, full plate," I interrupted, "it's way too much for one person. When will you have *Wanda time?*"

"That's true," she seemed to agree, "but I do love New Jersey. I guess I could try it and see if it worked with my schedule. Okay, I'll do it."

"Do what?" I demanded.

"Be your third *tour-guide-thingy*," she answered.

"I'm sorry," I said, waving my hands like a dizzy traffic cop, "did you say *tour-guide-thingy*?"

"I'm sorry," she replied in her usual sarcastic tone, "is the proper term *royal-tour-guide-thingy*?"

"T-Bone, can I have a word with you?" I asked as I grabbed him and slid him across the cafeteria floor. "Have you lost your mind? What are you doing? We work really hard to promote New Jersey and we're good at it. Now, you're begging her to help us like we don't know what we're doing. Need I remind you that there are bills to name us, *by name*, as Official Junior Ambassadors?"

"Nick, Nick, relax," he said as he straightened out his shirt. "Of course she won't be an Official Junior Ambassador like us. She'll be like a helper to me."

"Go ahead," I said.

"Go ahead what?" he asked.

"Go ahead and tell her that she's not gonna be an Official Junior Ambassador or a tour-guide-thingy," I said, pointing in her direction. "Tell her *she's* going to be *your* helper. I dare you."

As we returned to the spot where my day went really, really wrong and where Wanda stood, arms crossed, T-Bone slapped on his biggest smile. She was all business as she placed her hands on her hips. Poor guy, I thought.

"So, Wanda, Nicky and I would love your input and ideas. We'd like you to assist us in finding great places to visit. As my assistant, you could help New Jersey without it interfering with your schedule. What do you say?"

"Are you seriously asking *me* to be *your* assistant?" she asked, pointing at herself and then at T-Bone.

I was ready for the fireworks. Clearly, a co-president would never agree to be the other co-president's assistant anything. And clearly, Wanda's ego would never be comfortable being third banana.

"Only because I want you to be involved, but I don't want it to interfere with your grades or activities," he explained.

"Well, it *is* a good cause and being an assistant wouldn't interfere too much," she thought out loud. "Yes, I'll do it."

"We have a lot to discuss," he said, letting her walk in front of him and giving me a wink. When he pulled out her chair, I wanted to switch tables. Then I thought, *how long could this last*? For some reason, T-Bone aggravated her. Even though I was 99% sure *he* gave *her* the co-president thing, she still couldn't be nice to him. This couldn't last longer than a couple of weeks. I decided to ride it out.

Even though Wanda and her best friend, Dawn, were sitting across from us, very few words were spoken across the table. I was actually hoping the lunch-is-over-bell would ring. With three minutes to go, Wanda looked up and asked if we had plans for our next day trip.

"We always have something in the works," I assured her.

"Great," she said, stirring a pudding cup. "Where?"

"You want to know *where*?" I hesitated. "*Right now*?"

"Only if you know," she said, now deciding to make eye contact. Wanda was a human lie detector. She was like a combination parent, teacher, and principal in a kid's body.

"We have so many places," I told her, "that we'd need an extra lunch period to list them."

"Great," she said. "I'll stop by after school to see the list. But don't dilly-dally, I don't like it when people are late."

Don't dilly-dally getting home? She sounded like my grandmother. I looked at T-Bone, still staring at her.

"You realize I don't have a giant list ready?" I whispered. "What do I say when she comes over?"

"Tell her the list is in your head," he said. "That's what I always do. This way no one can prove if it's there or not."

18

"What if they ask you to tell them what's in your head? Then what, Einstein?"

"Why don't you make a list in study hall?" he suggested. "All you need is a list. That shouldn't be too hard."

I really had no other choice and needed to save face in front of *Little-Miss-Know-It-All*. I asked my study hall teacher if I could see a map of New Jersey and went to work. By the time the bell rang, I only had two things on the list. I couldn't believe it. Any other day, if you asked me to name great places we wanted to visit, I could name fifty of them. Now, because the new tour-guide-thingy challenged me, I was coming up dry. I knew it; she had gotten into my head. Maybe she was trying to force me out and take my spot. Each minute the pressure grew and my mind wandered. She made T-Bone fall in love with her and she made me paranoid. I always knew Wanda was trouble and now I had the proof. The only question left was *what to do about her?*

Chapter Three

By the time I got off the bus and arrived home, my heart was racing. I couldn't believe I needed to explain myself to Wanda. Before I could decide how to handle her, I could hear the front door open.

"Nicky, are you in here?" a strange voice asked.

As I approached the family room, I could see Wanda sitting on the couch.

"Did you ring the bell?" I asked. "I didn't hear it."

"No, T-Bone told me to go in and just make myself comfortable," she said as she pulled out a notebook.

"Of course he did," I said, hardly surprised.

"Where is T-Bone?" she asked.

"When we got off the bus, he said he had to run home," I told her. "He'll be here soon."

"So what have you got?" she said without looking up.

"I have to be completely honest, Wanda, our list is kind of confidential," I said. It was a brilliant, last-minute idea and I was proud of myself for thinking of it. "But I'd be happy to hear your ideas."

Why didn't I think of this before? There was no way Wanda could have prepared a list of ideas. Maybe this would prove that she wasn't qualified. We spend a lot of time researching awesome places. I was sure Wanda could never suggest anything valuable.

"Hey, guys," said T-Bone as he entered the family room. "Sorry I'm late. I had to run home and get something."

"Get what?" I asked, noticing a strong odor that followed him through the room.

"Uh, a pencil, I mean a pen, I mean, some money," he struggled to answer.

Wanda and I looked at each other, realizing T-Bone must have jumped into a bottle of his dad's cologne.

"What's that smell?" I asked.

"I don't smell anything," he answered, looking around the room and sniffing. "Can you describe the smell? Is it slightly woody and musky with a hint of manliness?"

"No, it smells like my grandfather," Wanda said as she wrinkled her nose.

Thinking this was a compliment, T-Bone said, "Oh, you must be enjoying my aftershave."

"Aftershave?" I laughed. "You ran home to put on some aftershave? You don't even shave."

Suddenly, his face was bright red. A really good friend would change the subject, but I couldn't help myself.

"Why are you so red?" I continued, thoroughly enjoying his embarrassment.

"Are you allergic to something?" Wanda asked as she examined his face and neck. "I think you have hives."

He didn't answer. For the first time, in a long time, T-Bone was speechless. I decided it was time to help him and I changed the subject. Plus, it was time to put the spotlight on Wanda and prove that she wasn't up to the job.

"Anyway," I began, "Wanda was about to share her New Jersey ideas with us."

"I'm happy to," she announced. "So, I've been reading your reports online and I think they're really good. My family has even visited a few of the places you suggested."

"Thanks," I said, not expecting Wanda to compliment us.

"You're welcome," she nodded. "My suggestion would be to promote New Jersey's natural beauty and wonder."

"Do you have anything in mind?" I asked.

"Yes, I do," she said. "New Jersey's Great Outdoors."

T-Bone and I sat there silently, waiting for her to finish her thought. She stared back at us. After two minutes of everyone staring, I figured she was finished.

"Wanda, I agree with you," I said. "New Jersey does have amazing outdoor places that most people don't even know exist, but what ones are you talking about? We can't just send our fans outside."

"Why not?" she asked.

"Because we pick specific places, visit them, write reports, post them on *our* website, and people visit those places," I explained. "We don't just tell them to go outside."

"Okay," she nodded. "I hear what you're saying. So, why not start with our state parks and forests?"

"Actually, we've visited several of them," I said. "We've visited the Delaware & Raritan Canal State Park, Washington Crossing State Park, Allaire State Park, High Point State Park, Stokes State Forest, and Fort Mott State Park, to name a few."

"There's a lot more," she smirked. "And besides visiting them, have you told people why they're so important?"

"Of course we have," said T-Bone, finally finding his voice. "They're really nice and fun."

"Obviously," she said, rolling her eyes. "But there's more. New Jersey's parks, forests, marinas, recreation areas, and historic sites are vital for the health of our state, *and they bring in money*."

"Go on," I said, surprisingly interested in her idea.

For the next hour, I was mesmerized. Wanda definitely did her homework. Not only did she seem to know about every inch of New Jersey's Great Outdoors, she also knew the history of most sites. Soon, we were clicking from site to site. I hated to admit it, but her idea was great. The best part was that we told her some things she didn't know.

"Have you ever heard of the Kuser family?" she asked.

"We wrote about them," I said. "They were very wealthy and very generous. They donated over 10,000 acres of land, their estate, and a monument to make High Point State Park; it was the largest land donation to New Jersey."

"Do you know what happened to the mansion?" she asked.

"Neglect!" T-Bone exclaimed. "The state let that mansion fall apart and then tore it down. That makes me so mad."

I remembered the day he read about the mansion at High Point and how angry it made him. I couldn't believe he was still so upset about it.

"Hold on," Wanda said softly, "before you attack the state, you should ask yourself *who the state is*. Remember, there are 121 people responsible for making New Jersey's laws and major decisions: forty senators, eighty members of the assembly, and one governor. But there are nearly nine million people that live here. If people were visiting that site and using their greatest weapons, that mansion would have never been torn down."

"*Weapons*?" asked T-Bone. "Like cannons?"

"Cannons?" I laughed. "Who uses cannons?"

"She said greatest weapon and I think cannons are great weapons," he replied. "Did you mean submarines?"

Wanda and I just looked at one another. I wished one of our trips could be inside T-Bone's head. I would have loved to get a closer look at how his brain worked.

"No, I'm not talking about those kinds of weapons," she said. "Maybe I should have said greatest tool."

"Like a hammer," T-Bone nodded.

"No, not like a hammer," she said. "Our greatest weapons are our voices, our time, and our money."

"My voice is definitely not my greatest weapon or tool," said T-Bone. "My mom says when I sing, animals hide."

"Let me try again," she began. "The 121 lawmakers represent the rest of us, you know, the almost nine million residents. They're elected to make decisions based upon what's best for the state and what the residents want."

"Sounds like a perfect plan," said T-Bone.

"It's hardly a perfect plan," she continued. "And while it's easy to blame politicians for everything and complain after a decision's been made, how many of the people complaining are informed and involved? *How many people are actually participating in government?*"

"Oh, me and Nick always say that," T-Bone exclaimed. "Remember I said that during the campaign?"

"That was a point I strongly agreed with," she admitted, "but this is bigger than student council and middle school. This totally affects New Jersey's future. As your assistant, I strongly urge you to promote our Great Outdoors."

I liked it. I liked it a lot. And I really liked the fact that *she knew she was his assistant*. I decided to start my research. The things I was reading about were fascinating and I started liking Wanda's idea more and more. When I found the Pocket Ranger app for New Jersey's State Parks and Forests, I was blown away. They really made the app interesting. You could look up the parks alphabetically, by region, or by activities. If you were looking for a great place to ride your bike, you'd click biking. Immediately, a link for every location that offered biking popped up.

As I explored the app, I found the usual activities, like hiking, biking, fishing, and kayaking, but there were more. There were so many activities that I never thought much about, like horseback riding, crabbing, kite flying, and swimming. I remembered our trip to Island Beach, also a state park. Then I found some unusual activities like dog sledding, ice fishing, ice sailing, and snowshoeing. I was shocked; they sounded like Alaskan activities.

I started clicking the names of random parks and forests. The more I clicked, the more I wanted to see. Each park had an overview, size of the park, history, activities, hours, directions, and any warnings. They couldn't have made it any easier to enjoy the great outdoors and I realized our job would be to promote the outdoors *and the app*.

By dinnertime, we had created a thorough list of places and an amazing list of connections. As much as we loved American history and knew how important New Jersey was to our country's birth and success, we hadn't given much thought to how much the country contributed to New Jersey. The more we searched, the more we learned.

"Hey, check this out," said Wanda as she pointed to the screen. "There's a book called *New Jersey State Parks, History and Facts*. It was written by a man named Kevin Woyce. I think we should download it."

"You mean buy it at the bookstore, right?" asked T-Bone.

"No, we can instantly download it," said Wanda. Two minutes later she pulled out her Kindle and started pressing buttons while she hummed. "There, now we have it."

"Just like that?" asked T-Bone. "We have the book?"

"Just like that," she said, cracking her first smile.

Neither one of us had a tablet or an e-reader; in fact, we didn't even have cell phones. Being the youngest in his family, T-Bone's mom said she learned the hard way about giving kids phones. Once, one of his brothers made a friend in Japan and ran up a $1,500 phone bill. T-Bone must have made her nervous because every time he asked for a phone, she pointed to the phone hanging on the kitchen wall. I didn't have a phone because my mom said I was unemployed. When I reminded her that I had my own business, she asked me if I was willing to spend $30 each month for a phone. After giving it some thought, it didn't seem worth it. The person I'd call the most, T-Bone, was always at my house anyway. This Kindle, though, seemed amazing. Just thinking about how much it could help me research and download books instantly made me even more excited about being an ambassador.

"Here," Wanda said as she handed it to me, "you can check it out while I do some more searching on the computer."

I was too embarrassed to tell her I didn't know how to

operate it, so I decided to wing it. I figured it couldn't be too hard if preschoolers could use them. I started tapping it and then turned it around several times. I closed the cover, opened it, and closed it again.

"What are you doing?" asked T-Bone.

"What does it look like?" I replied.

"Here, give it to me," he said, opening it up and jumping to the first page. "Swipe your finger across the screen."

Wow, I definitely needed to become more tech-savvy. Even T-Bone, often confused by his electric toothbrush, knew how to use a Kindle and a tablet.

My mom invited T-Bone and Wanda to stay for dinner and they both accepted her invitation. When my dad came home from work and saw two extra kids at the table, he took a second look. I think he was worried that Wanda was one of T-Bone's relatives.

"So are you kids working on a project?" my dad asked as he washed his hands and then headed toward the table.

"Kinda," said T-Bone. "Wanda and I are co-presidents and now she's assisting me with our New Jersey job."

"She's *your* assistant?" my dad asked with a broad smile. "*Really?*"

"Sure, Mr. A.," said T-Bone. "She's got some great ideas."

"Then maybe *you* ought to be *her* assistant," laughed my dad.

Before Wanda and T-Bone left, we told my dad some of our ideas about New Jersey's Great Outdoors. He agreed that we should promote the parks and forests. He agreed that the app was awesome. He even agreed to take us on some day trips. He did not agree, however, to buy me a Kindle. I decided three out of four wasn't too bad.

Chapter Four

While I dreaded including Wanda in the beginning, having her around wasn't too bad. She was organized, pretty handy with devices, and T-Bone was much quieter when she was around. As long as she stayed his assistant, I could live with the arrangement. After they left, I downloaded Kevin Woyce's book on our computer and started reading. I was amazed by the history of our parks and forests. Before Wanda's suggestion, I had never really thought about it, but now I wanted to know more.

At lunch the next day, we were really excited. Everyone had ideas and suggestions and they all sounded fantastic. I was so distracted by the great outdoors that I didn't mind when Wanda sat down at our table.

"Where's Dawn?" I asked, curious why her best friend wasn't sitting with her.

"She said I talked her ear off about New Jersey on the bus. She needed a break."

"I get that all the time," I laughed. "So I read something cool; did you know we didn't always have state parks?"

"Yeah, it was Theodore Roosevelt, the first conservationist president, that got the nature ball rolling," said T-Bone.

Wanda and I turned to look at him.

"What?" he shrugged. "I put that Kevin Woyce book on my mom's tablet and did a little light reading last night."

"I read it on my Kindle last night," said Wanda. "I also read that Kevin Woyce speaks about New Jersey and I printed his schedule. I think we should try to attend one of his appearances."

Much to my surprise, once again, Wanda had a great idea. For the rest of lunch and then after school, we plotted and planned our next adventures. The more I read, the more I couldn't wait to get started. The weather in New Jersey, from September through November, was especially great for spending time outdoors. It's when the summer heat and humidity, the same heat and humidity that makes beach days so awesome, slowly drifts away. Unless, of course, there's an Indian Summer. Ask any senior citizen and they'll tell you stories about Indian Summer, the weather phenomenon that extends heat and humidity through the fall season. But there was no Indian Summer this year. It was the beginning of October, and there was no better time to hike and bike.

T-Bone really wanted to explore Batsto Village in the Wharton State Forest. The history was fascinating, as it was once a town surrounding an iron ore furnace. We had already explored similar villages, and the combination of the great outdoors, and history was perfect.

Wanda suggested the Brendan T. Byrne State Forest. She said it had a very interesting history and former governor Brendan Byrne was an important part of its preservation. I wondered if we'd run into him when we visited.

I recommended Ringwood State Park. My research told me this park was a winner, too. There were two mansions and a botanical garden. It sounded amazing.

Other sites were added to the list, and they had some very interesting names: Cheesequake, Farny, Allamuchy Mountain, Double Trouble, Jenny Jump, Hacklebarney, and Wawayanda. The list went on and on. These names were so awesome; I decided I should write a song about them. I started humming and rhyming.

I hiked the trails at Hacklebarney,
Rode my bike real fast at Farny,
Reached the top of good ol' Barney,

Now, I just need one more word to rhyme with –*arney*.

Next, we checked out the marinas, recreation areas, and historic sites. To see so many places, we'd have to use weekends and after school. With days growing shorter, homework, and student council for T-Bone, our schedules would be tight. Then, a thought occurred to me. Could we possibly let Wanda help plan these trips and not invite her?

Now that she was involved, would she have to come? I was just getting used to the co-presidency thing. I was just getting used to her assisting. I was just getting used to her being in my house. I didn't think I could get used to bringing her along. How could I ask her not to come without looking mean? So far, she had been okay, and I really didn't want to hurt her feelings. I decided to ask my grandfather for his opinion. While I was at it, I'd ask him to bring us on some of these trips, too.

As I expected, when I called my grandfather, he was very excited. He considered himself quite the outdoorsman. Even though he was older than most people I knew, he was in better shape than most of them. Even better, he had been to several of these sites. He asked where we planned to go first and I suggested Batsto Village. He said it was a fine choice, and I loved a town built around a furnace.

Before we hung up, I asked him what I should do about Wanda. I explained the whole situation: smart girl, pretty nice, smells like a strawberry, politically aware, oh, and T-Bone was in love with her.

"Why do you feel so strongly against her coming?" he asked. "It sounds like you think she's a nice girl."

"She's a very nice girl," I agreed with him. "They have their co-presidency thing, and that's great. But this is our thing, and we've been working very hard at it. Why should she just jump in and be an ambassador now?"

"That's interesting," he said.

"What is?" I asked.

"It wasn't that long ago when you wanted every kid in New Jersey to join you and Tommy as ambassadors. Have you changed your mind about that?"

"No," I replied, "I do want kids all over New Jersey to join us. That's the best thing for our state. I just don't want her *to be us*."

"You have a point," he said. "She probably doesn't know half of what you boys know about the state. That could be a problem."

"Actually, she knows a lot," I told him. "Did I mention she was smart?"

"Yes, but even if she knows a lot about the ol' Garden State, I'm sure she couldn't plan trips and do the research like you boys."

"No, the whole great outdoors thing was her idea," I replied. "She even gave us the name of a book that was filled with great information."

"Hmmm," he hesitated, "even so, if Wanda and Tommy are in love, you'd have to watch them making puppy-dog eyes at each other. I'm with you; no one wants to watch two middle-school kids swooning over one another."

"Funny thing about that," I explained, "she doesn't give him the time of day. T-Bone's the only one swooning. It's actually kind of funny to watch him fall all over her while she ignores him."

"It's up to you, Slugger," he said. "Will it really help New Jersey to have someone else tagging along?"

"It might help," I reconsidered. "And we did want every kid to become an ambassador."

"Okay, then," he said, "I'll pick the three of you up bright and early Saturday morning."

"Thanks, Pop. Sounds good. See ya," I said as I hung up.

A few minutes later, I replayed our conversation in my head. I couldn't believe it; he did it again. My grandfather had a crazy way of making me change my mind simply by asking questions. He did it again, and I actually defended Wanda.

Saturday morning everyone met on my front porch. As I opened the door, Wanda was staring at the cars and T-Bone was staring at Wanda. When my grandfather pulled up, I automatically grabbed the front seat. After I sat down, I realized T-Bone would have to share the backseat with Wanda. It was the most awkward backseat ever and for some reason, that made me smile. For a moment, I couldn't remember why I didn't want her to come.

"So, I did some research and Batsto Village is pretty impressive," I said, beginning my usual pre-visit briefing.

"Actually, so did I," Wanda interrupted. "Batsto's history is really, really interesting. According to the Division of Parks and Forestry's website, Wharton State Forest is the largest single tract of land within the State Park System. Batsto is located in the forest and was a former bog iron and glassmaking industrial center from 1776 to 1867. It reflects the agricultural and commercial enterprises that existed here during the later 19th century."

Oh yeah, now I remember why I didn't want her to come. Even though she was nice and smart, she was clearly used to being the center of attention. She liked to take right over. It was time to take a stand.

"Very good," I smiled, not letting her see that she was getting on my nerves. "Did you know that this Pine Barrens village consists of…"

"Thirty-three historic buildings and structures, including the Batsto Mansion, gristmill, sawmill, general store, workers' homes, and post office," she interrupted again.

"And you can take a…" I said quickly, in an attempt to finish one sentence.

"Guided tour using your cell phone," she cut me off *once more*. "Using a walking brochure, the cell phone tour highlights eighteen historic sites and buildings in the village. Pre-recorded messages are two to three minutes long, and the tour is free. Isn't that great?"

"And there's a child-friendly museum," I blurted out so fast it sounded like *frueseum*.

"That's great, Nick," said T-Bone, smiling wildly at her, "but it looks like Wanda did the heavy lifting on this one."

What? Wanda did the heavy lifting? She printed the same page I had in my hand. She just spoke quicker and forgot a little thing called manners. It was all coming back to me. Little-Miss-Know-It-All just couldn't help herself. My grandfather saw what was happening and winked.

"So what can we do when we get there?" asked T-Bone.

I decided to let Wanda answer, but the car remained silent. Maybe she realized how obnoxious she was and decided to be quiet for a minute. I was afraid to open my mouth, but I figured enough time had gone by.

"We can start at the Visitors Center and take the…" I said.

"The cell phone tour and then check out the trails," she interrupted once more. "We should also talk to the State Park Police and get some good, solid data."

I couldn't believe how rude she was. Even my grandfather noticed and shook his head. *I felt bad for the Park Police.*

As soon as we parked the car, I noticed a man in a uniform. Apparently, Wanda caught a glimpse of him, too. Before I could even close my door, she was approaching him. Wow, she was pushy.

"Excuse me," she said, "are you a park police officer?"

He turned with a giant smile and said, "No, my name is Greg McLaughlin and I'm a Division Forest Firewarden. I'm not a police officer, but I may be able to help you. Do you have a question?"

"I do *now*," said T-Bone. "Is the forest on fire?"

"No," he smiled. "I'm happy to report that it's not on fire."

"Then why are you here?" T-Bone continued. "You're a fireman, right?"

"I'm a wildland or forest firefighter," he said. "But I'm not here to put out a fire. I'm here checking things out."

"Like what?" I asked.

"Well, being a wildland firefighter involves many things besides fighting fires," he explained. "We're responsible for many things like monitoring conditions, prevention, fire suppression, and maintaining equipment."

"Wow, that's awesome," said T-Bone. "What's it mean?"

"You're right, it is awesome," Greg laughed, "and very, very important, too. We monitor conditions and let people know if it's safe to have things like a campfire, and we post the risks on our signs and website. Fire prevention is a really big job. It involves hands-on activities like removing brush and setting prescribed burns as well as meeting with groups and individuals to teach them."

"Hold on," said Wanda, "are you saying you set fires?"

At least I wasn't the only one she interrupted.

"Well, our forests and these trees are more than beautiful things to look at; they're important to the health and safety of our entire state. Prescribed burns help prevent and contain forest fires."

"Hey, is that where the expression *fight fire with fire* came from?" I laughed.

"Everyone knows you fight fire with water," said Wanda.

"Actually," Greg smiled. "In the forest, you do fight fire with fire. I've always heard the expression originated in the 1800s when Settlers would guard against grass or forest fires by purposely starting small controllable fires, called backfires. They did this to remove flammable material in advance of a larger fire to deprive it of fuel."

"What if the fire you start gets so big that you can't put it out?" asked T-Bone.

"That's where the monitoring comes in," he explained. "We have to carefully watch things like temperature, humidity, and the most important one, wind. You see, wind can instantly change the direction of a fire, even a prescribed burn, and the effects can be disastrous."

"Does it really work?" I asked.

"Yes," he smiled. "A well-planned and well-controlled fire will burn up the fuel that could make a forest fire devour hundreds to thousands of acres. Think of a prescribed fire like you think of prescribed medicine from your doctor. The doctor prescribes medicine to keep you healthy, and we prescribe fires to keep the forest healthy."

"I'm sorry," said Wanda. "I always thought forest fires were bad. Doesn't Smokey Bear tell us that *only we can prevent forest fires?*"

"That's right," he agreed. "Smokey has been promoting forest fire safety since 1944. And we want people to know how to prevent forest fires. Those prescribed burns clear away the dead trees and vegetation, making room for new trees. It's part of a pretty important cycle."

"Oh, like when you trim your hair?" asked Wanda.

"Not a bad comparison," he nodded.

"How do you stop the fires you prescribe?" I asked. "I just realized you don't have hydrants out here."

"That's a good observation," he said as a man approached. "Guys, this is Steve Holmes. He's also a Firewarden and he works with me. I'm sorry; I didn't get your names."

"I'm T-Bone, this is Nicky, this is Wanda, and this is Pop," said T-Bone. "We're the soon-to-be Official Junior Ambassadors of New Jersey and Wanda is my assistant."

"So what do soon-to-be Official Junior Ambassadors do?" asked Greg.

"We find, visit, and report on great New Jersey places and then other people visit those places," I explained. "Right now, we're focusing on New Jersey's Great Outdoors."

"That's pretty awesome," Steve nodded. "But I hope while you're getting people excited to visit the great outdoors that you'll also tell them how to protect them."

"Definitely," said T-Bone. "We'll definitely teach people how to protect them. Oh yeah, one thing; how do we protect them?"

"I'll tell you what," said Steve, "if it's okay with Greg and Pop, you can meet us at the Brendan Byrne State Forest tomorrow, and we can tell you why they're important, why people should visit, and how to keep them safe."

"Really?" I asked, looking at my grandfather.

"I happen to be free tomorrow," Pop said with a smile.

"Okay, here's my card. Call me in the morning and I'll tell you where to meet," said Greg. "Is ten o'clock okay?"

I was hoping Wanda would be busy at dancing school or gymnastics *or climbing Mount Everest*, but like the rest of us, she was available. Just when I thought I couldn't take another minute of her talking, she surprised me once more.

"Here you go, Nicky," she said as she handed me three sheets of paper. "I'd give them to T-Bone, but I'm guessing you handle all of the paperwork."

"What's this?" I asked.

"It's the notes I took while everyone was speaking," she said with a smile. Somehow she managed to write down the entire conversation, *and it was neat*.

"Thanks," I said, somewhat stunned. As I turned to place the papers in my binder, she moved a little closer.

"I'm sorry for interrupting you earlier," she began. "I hate to admit it, but I was very excited to be invited and I didn't want you to think I was some sort of a slacker. I may have been trying too hard. I hope you'll accept my apology."

"That's all right," I replied, relieved that she noticed. "Don't worry about it."

Who would have ever thought *Wanda Know-It-All Heiss* would have a warm side? Definitely not me.

We headed to the Visitors Center/Museum and I grabbed the map and guide. I wanted to check out the Batsto Village and also some of the trails.

"Nick, Nick, Nick!" T-Bone shouted from the other side of the building. "They have a ghost town here. How awesome is this forest? They have a ghost town."

I looked at the park map and read about another village called historic Harrisville. Today, it's the remains of a company town, isolated deep in the Pine Barrens from the 1800s. Once a flourishing village, it was abandoned in 1891 after the great paper mill went out of business.

"Do you think they have ghosts?" asked T-Bone. "Do you think it's haunted?"

"Seriously?" asked Wanda. "You really think a ghost town has ghosts and is haunted?"

"Oh, that's nothing," I laughed. "He once asked me if the New Egypt Speedway was a jail for people who speed."

"Then what's a ghost town?" he asked.

After five attempts by my grandfather, we were able to explain that this was a busy town centered around a paper mill. Everyone who lived there was connected to the mill. When the mill went out of business, there were no jobs for people tucked so deeply in the forest and they had to relocate and find new jobs.

"They just left the town?" he asked. "I don't get it. Who leaves a town? No one stayed? Remember the Roebling Village? When they went out of business people didn't abandon the town. If I would have lived in Harrisville, I would have stayed and elected myself mayor."

"You'd last a week," my grandfather laughed, "right until the food ran out. And don't forget, the Roebling Village was in a more urban and accessible area. When the factory closed, people could find jobs nearby. The residents of Harrisville probably weren't that lucky."

"There's also an Atsion Village, with an Atsion Mansion," Wanda read from her guide. "It was the summer home of Samuel Richards, a Philadelphia ironmaster and operator of the Atsion furnace along the Mullica River. He died in 1842 and his family sold the property to another Philadelphia merchant named Maurice Raleigh. His family was the last to live in the mansion. When Joseph Wharton bought the property in 1892, he used the mansion for packing and storage for cranberry production. The state acquired the property in 1955."

"Wow, another furnace?" I said. "It says here the mansion appears as it did in 1826, with no plumbing, electricity, or heat other than from fireplaces, and it's unfurnished. If you call ahead, you can even take a tour."

"I'm just glad they didn't knock it down," said T-Bone, still upset about the neglect and demolition of the Kuser Mansion at High Point.

We started walking through Batsto Village and I did what I always do: I tried to envision a village filled with families, kids, and workers. The more I thought about it, I remembered driving by the Atsion Recreation Area's beach on Route 206 south.

"So here's some information about Batsto Village," said Wanda. "I got this from their website. During the iron-making and glassmaking periods, there were hundreds of people working and living there. They all needed homes in which to live. A sawmill was necessary to cut lumber for building homes. The gristmill was built for processing grain. The corn was kept in a nearby corncrib. A storage place for the processed grain was needed. Products that were not naturally available had to be purchased, therefore, a general store was built. The blacksmith was a necessary part of the community, as was a wheelwright. Different types of barns were erected for storage of wagons, equipment, and to house animals. The workers planted gardens and orchards. They raised animals for food. A piggery was built for slaughtering the pigs. Without refrigeration, an icehouse had to be constructed. Religion was important to the workers so churches were built nearby. Eventually, a post office helped to speed communication between Batsto and other towns."

As we walked through the village, we could see how they thought of everything. When we walked past the post office, it looked like it was still open. As I read the guide, it stated: *This is one of the four oldest post offices currently operating in the US. Opened in 1852 by Jesse Richards, one of Batsto's most prominent ironmasters, it served the community for many years. It closed in 1870 when the local economy failed. It reopened in the 1880s and closed in 1911. It was reopened by the Batsto Citizens' Committee in 1966. As a historical structure, it was never assigned a zip code. All stamps are hand-canceled.*

We used the cell phone audio tour and our maps to learn about each building. I was excited to tour the mansion. It must have been amazing to live in such a beautiful house. Wanda told us that in 1766, Charles Read founded the Batsto Iron Works. They made cooking pots and kettles and supplied wares to the Continental Army during the Revolution. In 1784, William Richards became a major owner of the iron works and continued manufacturing.

Iron production fell into decline in the mid-1850s and Joseph Wharton, a Philadelphia businessman, purchased Batsto in 1876, improved the mansion and other buildings on the property, and purchased a great deal of other property in the area. Wharton died in 1909, and the properties were managed from then until the mid-1950s by the Girard Trust Company in Philadelphia.

I wondered what it would have been like to start a whole village. It had to be hard without modern conveniences like telephones, cars, and electricity. During our guided tour we learned that the thirthy-two room Mansion, at the heart of the village, served as the former residence of generations of ironmasters and reflects the prosperity enjoyed during Batsto's industrial years. In the late 19th century, the structure was renovated into the elegant Italianate style of architecture by Joseph Wharton.

We were able to tour fourteen rooms, including the parlors, dining room, library, and bedrooms. It was like stepping back in time. My favorite room was the dining room with its long table that was set for dinner. Even though I knew no one was coming to dinner, I couldn't help but wonder how many important or famous people had dined there.

The house was much bigger than everything else, and the ironmasters' families must have enjoyed living in such a fancy home. It was a little sad. This village had once been so busy, and now it was so quiet. Thankfully, some good people had the sense to preserve it.

We walked through the village as I read about the Batona Trail. It was fifty miles long and connected Wharton, Brendon T. Byrne, and Bass River State Forests. I had to hand it to T-Bone; he definitely picked a good site.

"How big do you think this forest is?" I asked. "I need your answer to be in acres."

"10,000," said T-Bone.

"50,000," guessed Wanda.

"Pop, any guesses?"

"I'm going big," he said, "100,000 acres."

"Wrong, wrong, and close," I laughed. "It's 122,880 acres. That's huge."

"So what else can families do here?" asked T-Bone.

"Well, they have a lot of camping, from primitive sites to nine cabins," I read. "They also have canoeing, boating, wildlife observation, hiking, biking, cross-country skiing, fishing, kayaking, hunting, horseback riding, nature tours, historic tours, and snowmobiling."

"If you can't find something here to make you happy," said my grandfather, "then you just don't want to be happy."

"What time is it?" asked T-Bone. He suddenly realized it was past noon and that meant it was past his lunchtime.

"Are you kids hungry?" asked my grandfather.

"Starving," I answered, "but I doubt forests have diners."

"But your town has a WaWa," he smiled as he opened up his backpack. "Now, kids, here's the deal: the state parks and forests have a Carry-In/Carry-Out rule. So I stopped at WaWa and bought hoagies, chips, and drinks. When you're done, all leftover food and wrappers go back in my bag. Get it? Whatever you carry in, you carry out."

"Got it, Pop," I said. "And thanks for lunch."

After our picnic lunch, we did some more hiking. I was

impressed with how well my grandfather kept up. It was amazing. He really made me believe that age is just a number. The drive home was quiet. I was exhausted, Wanda was busy writing in her notebook, and T-Bone was staring at Wanda. When we arrived home, I emailed our friend, Billy at the State House to fill him in on our *new* New Jersey project. He loved the idea and couldn't wait for more reports. I couldn't wait for the next morning so we could meet with Steve and Greg. Unfortunately, for me, *Wanda couldn't wait either.*

Chapter Five

The next morning took forever to arrive. I figured it was because I was so excited. When I walked downstairs I could hear T-Bone and Wanda talking to my mom.

"Good morning, sleepyhead," said T-Bone. "Ready for our next adventure?"

As I got closer, I did a double-take. He was wearing white pants tucked into his white socks, a white long-sleeve shirt, a white bandana, white gloves, and an orange hat.

"What are you supposed to be?" I asked, examining his costume. "It's not too cold out; be careful you don't melt."

"He's not a snowman," said Wanda, rolling her eyes.

"Safety cone on top of a cloud?" I guessed again.

"No, he read an article about being safe in the woods. Apparently, his mom is letting him borrow her tablet and he's now researching everything."

I looked at my mom and she just shook her head and smiled. By now, she was used to T-Bone's quirks.

"What exactly is this *get-up* protecting you from?" I asked.

"According to the internet, if you walk into the woods you should protect yourself from insects, the sun, all poisonous leaves, and branches by wearing a safety outfit," he began. "Wearing white reflects the sun and you can easily spot insects, like tics. Pants tucked into my socks means bugs won't crawl up my leg and long pants and sleeves protect my skin from sunburn, poison ivy, and bug bites."

"And the bright orange hat?" I asked.

"All hunters wear bright orange hats for safety," he answered.

"But you're not a hunter, and it's not hunting season," I quickly replied.

"But orange must be the safest color," he said as he nodded and smiled. "You see, Nick, I'm always thinking."

When he asked me if I wanted to go change into a safety outfit, I didn't even answer him. I just walked over to the counter and grabbed a banana.

"Good choice," he said.

"What?" I asked.

"A banana is a good shot of potassium. My mom says it can stop you from fainting," he explained. "I read that on the internet, too, which means it must be true."

Oh, boy, I thought. Today was definitely going to be interesting. He acted like he drank fourteen cups of coffee and was hyper with caffeine. Instead, he was hyper with information. I heard the front door and footsteps heading our way. I wondered what my grandfather would say.

"Good morning," he said as he kissed my mom on the cheek. "You kids and the marshmallow ready to go?"

T-Bone started to laugh wildly until he realized he was the marshmallow. As we started driving, I was just about ready to read the information I had printed. Before I started to read, I turned and looked at Wanda. "Did you want to tell us anything about the site first?"

"No, I'm good," she smiled. "I'm sure you've got this."

"Okay, so the Brendan T. Byrne State Forest," I began, excited to have my job back, "was once called Lebanon State Forest. Today's forested acres are a strong contrast to the cleared land that existed in the 1800s. From 1851 until 1867, the very successful Lebanon Glass Works operated there. Guess why they shut down?"

"Because glass is dangerous?" said T-Bone. "Although it's strong, beautiful, and safe in a microwave."

"No, it's because they used all of the wood necessary to operate the furnace," said Wanda. When I looked at her funny, she said, "What? I never said I didn't read it too?"

"Anyway," I continued, "hiking is also a popular activity. Remember the famous Batona Trail connecting Wharton, Brendan T. Byrne, and Bass River State Forests? A typical through-hike along the trail takes approximately three days. There are over twenty-five miles of marked trails throughout the forest. In addition, the Mount Misery trail allows visitors the option of mountain biking, while the Cranberry Trail is wheelchair accessible."

"Wow, three days!" said T-Bone. "That's a lot of walking. Do they have hotels every eight miles?"

"No," I said.

"But they do have hotels?" he asked.

"Again, no," I said.

"No Hampton Inns and complimentary breakfast?"

"Once more, no," I said very firmly.

"Nearby, Whitesbog Village is another attraction," I read aloud. "It's been a major cranberry farm for over 120 years. At the turn of the 20th century, Whitesbog was the largest cranberry farm *in the country*. In 1916, Elizabeth C. White, with Dr. Frederick A. Coville, successfully developed the first cultivated blueberry."

"Today, the village has been preserved by the efforts of the Whitesbog Village Trust, and the cranberry bogs and blueberry fields still produce bountiful harvests. Visitors can see the semi-restored company town and walk among the bogs. The Whitesbog General Store is still open, selling blueberry and cranberry preserves, honey, and candies."

"Can you camp there?" asked T-Bone.

"Actually, Brendan Byrne State Forest is well known for its excellent campgrounds," I replied. "Unlike Wharton State Forest, all campsites are easily reached by car."

"That's so cool," said T-Bone. "One day, I'm gonna have a camper and I'm gonna live in the great outdoors."

"Live in the great outdoors or vacation there?" I laughed, doubting T-Bone could survive in the wild.

After giving it some thought, he decided he should probably just vacation in the woods. I continued providing details as we got closer.

"Ninety-three percent of the land within Brendan Byrne State Forest is open for hunting and trapping. Hunting is allowed during specific seasons, and bow hunting for deer is one of the most popular sports. During hunting season it's advisable to wear blaze orange or other brightly colored clothing to make yourself visible."

"Ah-ha!" T-Bone yelled. "See, blaze orange makes you visible. Who looks silly now?"

I turned around, looked at the giant, human cotton ball in the back of my grandfather's car, and decided that question really answered itself.

"Well, I think that's it," I said, concluding my briefing.

"Can I add something?" asked Wanda.

"Sure," I said, thankful she waited until I was done.

"Do you know why it was named Brendan Byrne State Forest?" she asked.

"Because Brendan Byrne was a governor," I answered.

"You're partly right," she replied, excited that she knew something we didn't know. "In the 1970s, numerous lawmakers and business leaders planned on developing the Pine Barrens. Their plans included turning the area into a

56

large city. They were discussing an airport, highways, homes, and businesses."

"Hold on," said T-Bone as we got closer to the forest. "They wanted to cut all of these trees down and make a city? That's the dumbest thing I've ever heard."

"That was the plan," she continued. "At the time, people were thinking about immediate rewards. They weren't really considering how losing the Pine Barrens would affect the whole state. Business people wanted to make money, and politicians need money from business people to support their elections and win campaigns."

"But who would take money for their campaign if they knew they'd have to make bad decisions?" asked T-Bone.

I thought the sip of coffee my grandfather took would come shooting through his nose. When he stopped gagging, he explained that this was exactly the reason we need to participate in government. He told us that it was our obligation to know what lawmakers were considering and use our voices. When we asked him how we could have a louder voice than rich businesspeople, he had a great answer.

"As individual voters, that's difficult, but as a group of educated voters, it's not," he explained. "You use your voice and your vote to let politicians know what they should or shouldn't do. And you use your wallet to let businesses know what they should or shouldn't do."

"Hmmm, I never thought about it like that," I said. "Strength in numbers, huh?"

"While many politicians claimed they wanted to preserve the Pine Barrens, Governor Byrne was the only person who did anything," said Wanda. "When he had a hard time getting enough lawmakers to vote for preservation, he wrote Executive Order 56 to stop development. He signed the Pinelands Protection Act in 1979, creating the nation's first National Reserve, and has consistently been a strong advocate of protecting this natural resource."

"He must have been a huge fan of the pinelands," I said.

"No," said Wanda, "I read an article on philly.com and it turns out the governor read a book called *The Pine Barrens,* written by John McPhee. Governor Byrne said that until he read the book, he knew very little about that wilderness area."

"You mean he was that inspired by a book?" I wondered.

"Yes," Wanda continued, "he was that inspired."

"That's great, but did he do it?" asked T-Bone. "Was he able to save the forest? Did they end up making the city?"

"You see the trees, don't you?" I asked. "And the signs that say Entering Brendan T. Byrne State Forest?"

"T-Bone, he preserved and protected nearly one-fifth of New Jersey's landmass," added Wanda. "They say it was his signature legislation and proudest achievement in office."

T-Bone was relieved. He decided he wanted to meet Governor Byrne and thank him. I doubted we would ever cross paths with a former governor and tried to convince him to write a letter. I even suggested giving the letter to our friend, Billy. He worked in the governor's office and I was sure he could get the letter to Governor Byrne. T-Bone considered it and decided he needed to meet him.

We pulled into the forest and saw Greg and Steve standing by the Welcome Center. I had so many questions to ask them, including the one I'd probably be too nervous to ask: if we could climb to the top of the fire tower. They were happy to see us and brought us right inside. We were introduced to a woman working behind the counter, and I spotted a wall filled with maps and park guides.

We excitedly headed to the forest. Greg explained what underbrush was and pointed out how the low bushes, leaves, and grasses can fuel a fire. He said a wildfire is unpredictable and susceptible to weather conditions, but a prescribed burn is the safest way to remove brush and undergrowth and reduce hazardous fuels.

I still wondered how healthy it could be for a forest to be on fire, but they explained that wildlife thrives after a burn and the forest floor returns to a proper natural balance. We learned that it releases nutrients and allows light into the forest and regeneration of native plants that feed wildlife. If the forests are not burned regularly, leaf litter and shrubs accumulate, starving wildlife and creating the risk of uncontrollable wildfires.

I figured it was kinda like spring cleaning at home. If we didn't remove things from the floor, there could be trouble. I still didn't understand how they controlled a fire. It seemed impossible, especially without fire hydrants.

Steve told us that there were fire seasons and surprisingly, summer wasn't one of them; most fires occurred in the spring and fall seasons. He said they conduct prescribed burns during the cooler months to reduce fuel buildup and decrease the chances of hotter fires. Controlled burning stimulated germination of forest trees and renewed the forest. I was shocked that controlled fire was a tool.

"When we talk to kids we make sure they understand that *fire is only a tool when it's used by professionals, properly planned, and the right equipment is on hand,*" cautioned Greg. "Forest fires are deadly, dangerous, and expensive."

"I try everything possible to avoid fire," said T-Bone. "One time, I sensed the fire on our grill was getting too high and threw a bucket of water on it."

"Your dad must have been proud," said Greg.

"He probably would have been prouder if I had waited until he got the steaks off the grill first," T-Bone shrugged.

Steve looked at T-Bone and rolled his eyes. I sometimes forgot that new people weren't used to him. Luckily, they had so much to share, they quickly forgot about him.

"I wrote down a bunch of questions," I said. "The first one is, what does your uniform look like?"

It's different than the uniform your local firefighters wear," Greg began. "We wear fire-resistant pants and shirts, hard hats, gloves, and heavy boots. We also carry pop-up fire shelters that temporarily reflect heat as a last resort."

"Last resort?" I asked.

"Sure, Nicky," he said. "Wildland fires are extremely dangerous, even those we are controlling. We take every fire seriously and prepare for as many situations as possible. Unfortunately, forest fires aren't simple to suppress or put out. We don't have a fire truck hooked up to a hydrant behind us, and the size of a forest fire can cover thousands of acres."

"It sounds really dangerous," I said. "If firefighters get in trouble, can they run?"

"Well," said Greg, "the biggest variable in wildland firefighting is Mother Nature. Nationally, we lose firefighters every year when wind gusts suddenly change direction or fuel buildup sparks explosions. Outrunning a fire? A horse couldn't outrun a fire."

"Wow, I had no idea," I said, shaking my head in awe. "Faster than a horse, huh?"

"I did," said Wanda. "A report from the National Wildfire Coordinating Group said from 1990-2006, 310 wildland firefighters died during firefighting operations."

"*Holy moly,*" said T-Bone, "that's a lot of people."

"And that's an improvement," Wanda continued. "I found some other interesting facts while reading their report. In 1871, the Peshtigo Fire burned more than 1.5 million acres in Wisconsin, killing more than 1,200 people. It wasn't until the Big Burn of 1910 killed at least seventy-eight firefighters and burned millions of acres in northern Idaho and western Montana that the people understood how serious they really are. Oh and there was a 1963 forest fire that burned 183,000 acres between Burlington County and the Atlantic Ocean with seven deaths."

Everyone looked at Wanda. "Too much?" she asked.

"Not at all," said Steve. "You did your homework."

"How about tools?" I asked, checking off my questions.

"Again, lots of differences," said Greg. "We actually use bulldozers, helicopters, special-built fire trucks, and small planes, and we carry hand tools like shovels."

"That's different than the tools the firefighters in Trenton showed us," I said, remembering our visit to Engine 1 and Ladder 1. "They use a lot of hose and a lot of ladders."

"Sure," said Steve. "They're fighting a different type of fire. They use the tools that help them get the job done, just like we do."

"What do you have to do if you want to be a wildland firefighter?" I asked. "Should you be a boy scout?"

"Well, you don't have to be a boy scout," Greg laughed, "but the skills boy scouts learn can come in awful handy. You see, when you fight this kind of fire, you're often not real close to the other firefighters, so you should definitely have some outdoor skills."

"If you're 18-years or older, you can apply to be a part-time wildland firefighter and training will be provided," added Steve. "If you want to be a full-time firefighter, you need a two-year degree in forestry or fire science. We look for individuals who are self-motivated, independent, and able to handle the physical demands of the job."

"Who gets to go to the top of the tower?" I asked, hoping it would spark an invitation.

"Oh," Steve laughed, "you mean the Fire Lookout Towers."

"Oh yeah, the Fire Lookout Towers," I nodded, trying to act cool. "They look interesting."

"Well, there's nothing fancy about them, but they offer some pretty amazing views," said Greg. "Would you like to check it out?"

Since last night, I was practicing my play-it-cool face in case they asked us to go up. If I let them know how excited I was, they might have had second thoughts. I furrowed my eyebrows and nodded thoughtfully. Steve asked me if something had just stung my face. Okay, I thought, maybe too much with the eyebrows.

As we climbed to the top, I was amazed by how physically fit my grandfather was. T-Bone was huffing and puffing more than he was. During our ascent, we learned some more interesting details. We learned the causes of forest fires are almost always people. I was shocked. I totally would have guessed lightning or sun or heat or all three. It turns out that humans are the greatest threat for forest fires, whether they are accidental or on purpose.

"Even more than sunlight through glass?" asked T-Bone.

"Even more," said Greg. "It can be a careless action, like not putting out a campfire properly or tossing a lit cigarette out of a car window, or disregarding regulations and posted warnings. Of course, there are also people who commit the senseless act of arson, which is purposely setting a fire."

"So, since people are the main problem," Wanda deduced, "then people can be the main solution, right?"

"Absolutely," said Greg.

"That's it," said T-Bone. "We're making this a *priority* priority. We have to make sure people protect New Jersey's Great Outdoors. We have to make sure every kid in New Jersey knows these things."

The view from the top of the Fire Lookout Tower was amazing and Tim, the fire observer, told us all about his important job The Pine Barrens are enormous and the longer fires burn, the stronger and more out of control they grow. That makes spotting them as soon as possible very, very important.

"What's the most dangerous part of the job?" I asked.

"The fire is definitely the most dangerous thing, right?" T-Bone guessed.

"Believe it or not, another great danger is traffic," said Steve.

"Are there highways in the forest?" asked T-Bone.

"No," he laughed, "it's more from pulling bulldozers, parking on the side of roads in thick smoke conditions, and motorists failing to be extra careful."

"I'd have never guessed traffic," I nodded. "Are wild animals another great danger?"

"No," said Greg, "believe it or not, animals sense fire and often leave the area in advance of the danger. Birds fly away, some animals go underground and wait for the danger to pass, while others evacuate. The next greatest danger is falling trees."

"Oh, I never thought of that," I said. "You've gotta be really brave to a wildland firefighter."

"That's very true," my grandfather agreed. "The men and women who protect our forests are truly unsung heroes. We often forget how hard they work, the challenges of this type of firefighting, and the dangers they face. They risk their lives to protect lives, property, and very, very valuable resources."

By the time we reached the ground, I was amazed at how much we had learned in such a short period of time. I was so interested in what Greg and Steve were telling me, I almost forgot Wanda was with us. They gave us their cards and invited us to contact them if we had any more questions. I told them we'd do a special report and post it on www.nickyfifth.com. They were happy to hear that.

Before leaving, they grabbed a shovel and dug a small line.

"What's that?" asked T-Bone curiously. "Are you planting a garden?"

"Excuse me?" Greg and Steve said at the same time.

"I'm actually pro-garden," said T-Bone. "It was part of my platform when I ran for student council president. I was thinking of school or community gardens, but I guess a forest garden might be a good idea, too."

"No, we're not digging a garden, we're digging a fire break," said Greg. "You see, if you dig 6-8 inches, you hit soil that doesn't contain burnable fuel. That can be enough to prevent a fire from spreading."

"Wow, that is pretty smart," said T-Bone. "Although a forest garden isn't a bad idea, either."

"Well, for stopping a fire it would be," Steve laughed.

We said goodbye and decided to explore the forest. With a map in hand, we were able to start hiking. The trails were marked, and we were able to take a long walk without getting lost. The sun felt good poking through the branches, and I realized I liked hiking. It was relaxing and energetic all at the same time. T-Bone started talking about hiking the Batona Trail, which led to him talking about the Appalachian Trail, which then led to him talking about walking across America. If I had a list of everything he planned to do, it would be *longer than the Batona Trail*.

When we took a break, my grandfather read about the Whitesbog Village, an early 20th-century-company town and agricultural community. Listed on both the National and State Registers of Historic Sites, it includes the village and the surrounding 3,000 acres of cranberry bogs, blueberry fields, sugar sand roads, and Pine Barrens' forests.

We drove over to Whitesbog and followed the driving tour. There were narrow paths throughout the bogs, and we could really appreciate the importance of the village. Wanda told us the village was open on weekends and that the General Store carried many blueberry and cranberry items. They even had festivals at the village.

"Well, Wanda," I said as I sunk into the front seat of my grandfather's car, "you definitely picked a winner."

"Thanks, Nicky," she said, "but it's hard not to pick a winner. It's just a matter of what you're looking for."

"That's true," said T-Bone. "And I forgot to tell you something earlier. When we were at the top of the Fire Lookout Tower, I asked Greg if we could visit other towers and he said we could. I'm pretty sure it's because I'm the co-president. I guess that's one of the perks of this job."

"That's funny," I said. "He told me anyone could go to the top if a fire observer is up there and invites you up."

"Not just anyone," T-Bone corrected. "I'm sure you have to be a dignitary or a politician, *like me and Wanda*."

"Nope," I shook my head. "Any family driving down the street can ask to go up."

"I'm sure you misunderstood," he insisted, "but don't worry, you'll be able to visit any tower you want."

"Oh, really? Why is that? Because anyone can?" I laughed.

"Of course, not," he said, "*because you know me!*"

Chapter Six

It was an exciting, but long, weekend and we had two major reports to write, plus a report about forest fire safety. I felt like I had learned so much and needed to tell every person in New Jersey. Of course, with almost nine million people in our state, personally delivering the message was a little unrealistic. My idea was to put it on our website and have as many people as possible read it. Then, if every person who read it told twenty people and each of those people told twenty people, before you knew it, we'd cover the whole state. It was my best idea, it worked in the past, and it was all we could afford. Translation: *it was perfect*.

It was pretty late Sunday night when the house phone rang. Since it wasn't so late that it had to be an emergency call and since I received approximately 1% of the telephone calls, I ignored it. A moment later, my mom was standing in my doorway.

"It's for you," she said with a grin. *"And it's a girl."*

I couldn't imagine who it could be. My mom and my sisters were home and if it was my grandmother or a relative, my mom would never announce that it was a girl.

I shrugged my shoulders and grabbed the cordless phone.

"Hello," I said.

"Nicky? It's Wanda."

Wow, I thought, she never even crossed my mind. It really was true: *out of sight, out of mind*.

"What's up?" I asked.

"Well, I know you mentioned doing your report tonight and I have some pictures and additional information you might find useful. Is it okay if I send it to you?"

"Sure," I said. "Send it to nickyfifth@nickyfifth.com."

"That's original," she replied with her typical sarcasm. She must have been holding in sarcastic comments all weekend, and she was probably close to bursting.

I ran downstairs to the computer and a moment later, her email arrived. This girl was nothing if not thorough. I opened her attachments and they were filled with great pictures, some that she had taken and some from the state website. As I opened the files, I thought I heard the phone ring. A moment later, my mom was standing in the family room, looking a little less chipper than the first time.

"Guess who it's for?" she asked, covering the receiver. *"Oh, and it's not a girl."*

"Hello," I said, sure I knew who was on the other end.

"Nick, Nick, it's me, T-Bone. Did Wanda just call you?" he asked in a panic.

"Yeah, why?"

"I knew it," he said. "I knew it. I knew she'd call you."

"How did you know she would call me?"

"Because she called me, asked for your number, and said she was calling you," he explained.

"That's a lot of deducing, Sherlock," I said in my most sarcastic tone. "You figured that out all by yourself and with so few clues. The only thing you had to go on was that Wanda called you, asked for my number, and told you she was calling me? How did you piece that all together?"

"I had a feeling," he said as the sarcasm flew quickly over his head. "I had a bad feeling."

"What bad feeling?" I asked.

"I think she loves you," he stammered, as if each word caused him enormous pain.

"What?" I shrieked. "Are you crazy? I mean, seriously, have you fallen off the ladder again? We barely speak and are only trying to get along because of you."

"That's the oldest story in the book, Nick," he said. "Hatred is a strong emotion, and hate can turn into love. It's a thin line, Nick; a very thin line. Don't you watch the classic movie channel? *C'mon, Nick, think!*"

"First of all, I don't hate her," I said, very slowly. "Second of all, she doesn't hate me. There are no strong emotions that will turn into love."

"Nick, you poor, dumb sap," he persisted, "you're too close to see it. Haven't you ever watched a Bing Crosby and Bob Hope Road movie? If you haven't, you should; they're hysterical. But anyway, Bing is always stealing Bob's girl, even when he isn't trying. You're Bing and I'm Bob. *Why, why, why can't I be Bing?*"

"And third of all, Bob," I continued, "she called to get my email address so she could email me pictures for the report. The call lasted about a minute, and I think we forgot to say goodbye before we hung up."

"Oh, was that all?" he asked as if it was nothing. "Um, scratch everything I said, unless you guys start to hate each other. Then remember it."

"Is that all you wanted?" I asked him.

"Pretty much," he said as he hung up the phone.

It took a lot longer to finish the reports because there was so much information to include. Luckily, my mom fell asleep and didn't realize I was still downstairs. It was well after midnight by the time I had wrapped up. The next morning was awful. I couldn't wake up, and I couldn't find anything I needed. I felt like that kid Alexander from the book about having a terrible, no good, rotten day that my mom used to read to us.

The bus ride seemed quicker than usual, although that may have been because I slept most of the way. As the bus stopped in the school parking lot, I could feel T-Bone pulling my eyelid open.

"Good morning, sleepyhead," he said, well-rested and ready to start his day.

For a moment, I was confused and didn't even know where I was. I barely made it through my morning classes. At lunch, I headed to our table in the cafeteria. I was so tired I didn't even feel like eating. That's when T-Bone and Wanda sat down next to me.

"So we went to Wharton State Forest and Batsto Village like T-Bone suggested," Wanda began. "And we went to the Brendan T. Byrne State Forest like I suggested, so I guess our next stop is Ringwood like you suggested."

"Huh?" I asked.

"Ringwood State Park," said T-Bone. "Wanda printed out some information and it looks awesome. When do you think we can go?"

"Go where?" I asked.

"Hey, Nicky," T-Bone waved his hands in front of my eyes. "Snap out of it. We're planning our next trip."

"Oh," I nodded. "The next trip."

"Is he okay?" Wanda whispered. "He doesn't look good."

She was right. I was exhausted. The schoolwork and homework, getting up early, and spending every other minute visiting great places or writing about them was catching up with me.

"I was thinking," she said, "we have off on Friday, maybe we should go then."

"Okay," I said, not realizing what I had just agreed to do.

"Great, here's the research," she said as she handed me a pink folder with a rainbow and neon stars.

"Okay," I repeated, placing the folder under my books.

When the bell rang, I grabbed my stack of books, totally forgetting about the bright pink, neon folder Wanda had given me. As I walked to my next class, guys I knew were pointing at me and laughing. It wasn't until I got in the classroom that I realized they were laughing at the folder. I quickly slipped it into my binder.

The rest of the week was sheer madness. I had reports due, quizzes, labs, and tests. When I got on the bus to go home Thursday, I leaned my head against the window. I decided I would sleep until Saturday; maybe even Sunday.

"So what time should we go?" asked T-Bone.

"Go where?" I mumbled.

"We have off tomorrow, remember, and we're going to Ringwood State Park," he replied.

"Going to, what, Ring-what, where?" I squinted as I questioned him.

"Nick, you have to get more sleep," he laughed. "You can't remember anything this week. You did ask your grandfather to take us, didn't you?"

"Ask my grandfather what?" I repeated. "We're going to Ringwood tomorrow?"

I had totally forgotten. It was slowly coming back to me, but I knew I never asked my grandfather.

"You did ask him, didn't you?" said T-Bone. He looked like a four-year-old waiting to find out if he was going to the circus.

"Oh yeah, sure, I forgot. He said okay," I told him.

Suddenly, I remembered Wanda's pink folder. As soon as I got home, I pulled it out. I read through everything and realized it wasn't only amazing, it wasn't real close. It was very close to the New York State line. I called my grandfather, hoping he wasn't busy. Luckily, his plans had changed and he would be able to take us.

The next morning, as I started heading down the steps, I could hear Wanda and T-Bone talking to my grandfather. I had no idea what time they all woke up, but it had to be pretty early for three people to beat me to my own kitchen.

"Feeling any better?" asked T-Bone.

"Yeah, a little," I lied.

"You know, I was thinking," said Wanda. "Since I'm already T-Bone's assistant, I could also be your assistant."

"What?" I asked, noticing T-Bone glaring at me.

"Well, you write all of the reports," she continued. "Would you like me to write them up and email them to you and T-Bone before you send them to Billy?"

"Hmmm," I stopped and thought for a moment. I wasn't sure if she genuinely wanted to help or if this was part of her evil plan to push me out of the equation. I still didn't trust her 100%, but on the other hand, it would help out a lot. "I guess you can, if you have the time."

T-Bone looked horrified. I was sure I'd get some kind of a speech later and figured something similar probably happened to Bob Hope in one of those Road movies. I was definitely going to have to watch them one day.

We headed north to Ringwood, and Wanda asked me if I wanted to read the background information.

"No, you did all of the work, so you should read it," I said, hopefully proving to T-Bone that I didn't hate her. It seemed to work, and I noticed him perk up a bit.

"So Ringwood was an excellent choice," she began. "It's located in Bergen and Passaic Counties and is a great place for families. According to my research, it has a little bit of everything. There's nature and history throughout the park with moderate to difficult trails, perfect for all hikers, horseback riding, and mountain biking. There's even a lake for swimming, and you can bring your raft or inner tube. You can even canoe, boat, or fish on the lake."

"That reminds me of Lake Marcia at High Point," I said, finally coming to life. "That was one of the best trips. My parents didn't tell us they packed our bathing suits and pretended to stumble upon this awesome mountain lake."

"That was awesome," T-Bone agreed. "How are the views?"

"According to the websites and books I checked out, the views are spectacular," she said. "And since you guys like history so much, there are two manors."

"Like *please* and *thank you*?" asked T-Bone. "Because I'm pretty sure there's more, like *you're welcome*, *I'm sorry*, *excuse me…*"

"Not manners," she interrupted for good cause this time, "I mean manors. Ringwood Manor is a beautiful country home and the home of ironmasters for almost 200 years. The other is Skylands Manor. It was built in the 1920s, has 44 beautiful rooms and large windows with 16th-century stained glass windows. You can tour them both."

"Hmmm, manors," T-Bone nodded, "that's a new one."

"No, not really," Wanda shook her head and kept reading. "So the Ringwood Manor was owned by Abraham S. Hewitt, America's foremost ironmaster. Ring any bells?"

"Is he friends with George?" asked T-Bone, referring to, George, a senior citizen who had become our good friend.

"Exactly how old do you think George is?" I laughed. "And yes, it's definitely ringing bells. There's a town called Hewitt and a park, no, a forest, yes, a forest, with a name like Abraham or Hewitt."

"Actually, there's a state forest called Abraham S. Hewitt State Forest," said Wanda.

"Wow, can you imagine a kid with a name like Abraham S. Hewitt living near a forest with that name?" T-Bone exclaimed. "That had to be awesome."

"No, no, no," said my grandfather, unable to take any more. "Abraham S. Hewitt State Forest is named *after* him. It wasn't a coincidence."

"Too bad," said T-Bone. "He'd be the most popular kid."

"Anyway," Wanda plodded through her notes, "in Kevin Woyce's book, I learned that Abraham Hewitt's story starts with a man named Peter Cooper. Cooper built the first steam locomotive in 1830 to talk the owners of the new railroad into using steam instead of horses. He made his fortune selling iron rails. Now, his forges were the first to burn anthracite coal instead of charcoal and he brought a method of purifying American steel to the USA in 1856, only a year after it was introduced in England."

"So this guy was smart and rich?" asked T-Bone.

"Yes and yes," said Wanda. "Hang on, it gets better. In 1858, he was the president of the New York, Newfoundland, and London Telegraph Company, supervising the laying of the first transatlantic telegraph cable."

"Pretty impressive," I agreed.

"It gets even better," she continued. "He was also a social reformer and philanthropist…"

"Ooh, that's what I'm gonna be one day," T-Bone interrupted. "I'm gonna give away millions of dollars to projects that help people."

"Projects won't be hard to find," my grandfather laughed, "and everything that helps people needs money."

"Not only was he generous, he campaigned against slavery before the Civil War and defended the rights of Native Americans, as well as supported public education. In 1859, he opened Cooper Union, a free, co-educational college of science, technology, and art in New York."

"That's pretty awesome," I said.

"Is *co-educational* like *co-president*?" asked T-Bone. "Is that where two educations work together?"

"No," Wanda corrected him, "co-educational meant it was open to male and female students."

"Oh," said T-Bone, "he sounds great, but what does he have to do with Abe?"

"Okay, in the 1840s, Cooper hired Hewitt, a Columbia University graduate, to tutor his son, Edward. Well, Edward and Abraham become lifelong friends and business partners. In 1845, they started the Trenton Iron Company. They were even mayors of New York City, Edward in 1879 and Abraham in 1886. Abraham also served several terms in the United States Congress."

"Did you hear that, Nick?" T-Bone winked. "Two friends both became mayors. I'll go first and I'll keep the seat warm for you."

"Anyway," Wanda tried to finish, "since their iron mill specialized in making railroad rails and they needed a steady supply of high-grade ore, they bought the Andover Mine for $2,500.00 in 1848."

"Wow, I could almost afford that!" exclaimed T-Bone.

"You wouldn't have that much money in 1848," I laughed.

"Now, the Ringwood Iron Works was started much earlier, in 1742," she continued, "and was bought and sold several times. It was crucial in providing supplies to the colonies during the Revolution. In 1807, according to the Kevin Woyce book, Martin Reyerson bought the property and built a ten-room mansion. He died in 1832, and his sons couldn't afford to keep it. Peter Cooper, the dad, and Abraham Hewitt bought it in 1853 for $100,000. When ore was discovered near the Great Lakes, the mine slowed down, finally closing in the 1950s."

"Hey, Pop, you were alive then," I blurted out.

"Thanks for the reminder, sport," he laughed and patted my head. "And before you ask, T-Bone, I did not know Cooper, Cooper, or Hewitt."

"Whatever happened to Hewitt?" asked T-Bone. "Did he die a rich, lonely man?"

"Hardly," said Wanda. "He married Peter Cooper's daughter, Sarah, in 1855. She fell in love with Ryerson's manor, so she and Abraham spent their lives remodeling and enlarging the home for their large family of six kids."

"Did he donate the ten-room manor?" asked T-Bone.

"No," Wanda laughed, "he donated the manor, that by 1936 had fifty-one rooms, twenty-four fireplaces, and over 250 windows."

"I'd hate to be their maid," said T-Bone. "That's a lot of windows to wash."

"I get it," I announced as the imaginary lightbulb over my head started flickering. "Hewitt donated his mansion and land and the state named the forest after him, right?"

"I love how it's all connected," said my grandfather. "And I love how you kids are doing your homework and finding some really interesting facts. So many amazing places and things in our state were only made possible by the donations of responsible, social-minded, wealthy families. They really felt that they had an obligation to give back."

"Did they make them give back?" asked T-Bone.

"No, but there was no income tax back then," Pop explained. "People kept more of their money, but they also gave away more. I remember my father telling me that from those who have much, much is expected. I never forgot that."

"I like it," I said, secretly hoping to one day be a captain of industry, creating jobs and innovative products, and then becoming a philanthropist. Having learned about what so many others achieved and gave back, I had a lot of ideas.

"Oh, one more connection," said Wanda, "The Ringwood Company donated their Long Pond property to the state in 1957 and thirty years later, the Long Pond Ironworks State Park opened. In 1999, the Friends of the Long Pond Ironworks State Park opened a museum and are even restoring some of the buildings."

"I'm definitely gonna be a friend when I grow up," said T-Bone, referring to the organizations that support various sites around the state.

We were a few minutes away from Ringwood when I realized that Wanda had missed something.

"Wanda," I called, "are you forgetting something?"

She quickly browsed through her notes and confirmed that she had, indeed, covered everything.

"How about the State Botanical Gardens?" I smiled.

"Oh, how could I forget that?" she said, covering her mouth. "It's only one of the largest gardens in New Jersey. There are thousands of plants, shrubs, and trees in over thirty gardens. Each garden was handcrafted and perfectly positioned for the best views."

"Good job," said my grandfather as he parked the car.

The air was crisp and we were eager to see the park, the botanical garden, and the manors. It made such a difference that we briefed ourselves before we went anywhere. If we would have just shown up, without any prior knowledge, we wouldn't have gotten too much out of it. Maybe the parents of kids who thought history and nature were boring should try it.

We walked through the gardens, and the description Wanda read didn't do them justice. The reflecting pool was very cool, almost as cool as the whispering bench. It was a long curved stone bench and if you sat at one end and whispered, a person on the other end could hear it clear as a bell. Of course, when we first tried it, T-Bone sat right next to me and whispered, "Can you hear this?"

"Geez, do you think?" I shook my head. "You're not supposed to whisper in my ear. We to sit at opposite ends."

After seven tries, he finally understood what to do. Wanda sat in my seat to take a turn, and T-Bone didn't realize. I wasn't sure what he said, but whatever it was, it made her jump up and turn red. It was probably about her hair again.

Everyone was anxious to see the manors, and luckily they were open for tours. A woman named Karen overheard our conversation and explained that some locations are not open every day. She was really nice and I wondered how she knew so much. It turned out that she worked for the

Department of Environmental Protection. She was really nice and told us about the police who protect our parks.

"You know, New Jersey's natural resources are extremely valuable," she said. "The Park Police protect *the parks and the visitors*; they're a vital part of the system."

I never thought about it, but it was true; there was so much area to cover. When she started to tell us about the wildland firefighters, we told her we had already met Greg and Steve. Surprisingly, she knew them very well.

"Have you been here before?" I asked her.

She smiled and said, "I've been here many, many times. Part of my job is to go to all of our state sites."

"No way!" said T-Bone. "Part of your job is to visit state parks and forests? That's awesome."

"It is awesome," she agreed. "When you work for DEP, you become a steward of our environment. That means we protect it."

When we told her about our jobs, she was really impressed and told us we were stewards, too. We asked her about the manors, and she said we'd love them. She was right.

The Skylands Manor was beautiful. It was part of the State Botanical Gardens and also a bed & breakfast. I couldn't believe people were allowed to stay there. The inside was like a church with thick wood molding, high ceilings, and even stained glass. The Skylands was like the game board from CLUE. It had a study, library, dining room, and even a grand ballroom. We met Eric Pain, the superintendent of the park, and Kristen Brandt, the visitor service assistant, when we walked toward the foyer.

Naturally, T-Bone told him who we were and they were happy to show us around. They showed us what a room looks like for the guests who stay over, and then we walked along the grounds.

"Do you think they had a gardener?" asked T-Bone.

"No," said Wanda, "I'm sure the rich owners came out themselves, with their push mowers and garden shears."

"Oh yeah," said T-Bone, "gardeners were probably too expensive."

"Too expensive?" she shrieked. "T-Bone, look at the size of this place. Do you really think someone could own a mansion like this and not be able to afford a gardener?"

"So, *you think they had a gardener*?" he asked again.

I stepped back in case Wanda slugged him. I wanted to make sure she didn't get me by accident. I also looked at Eric and Kristen's faces. It was always fun to watch people during their first *T-Bone encounter.*

"T-Bone, they probably had a gardener, a couple of cooks, caretakers, nannies, drivers, and assistants," she explained.

"Wow, they must have been rich," he said.

"Let's just look at the gardens," suggested my grandfather.

I wondered how it must have felt to wake up in the morning and look out your window to this view: a mansion and gardens in the forest. My grandfather said it would make any childhood magical, but it could have been lonely, too. He said very wealthy kids often had many restrictions, including who they could play with. Plus, a home this large was also isolated and didn't provide the same opportunities to make friends as kids who lived in regular neighborhoods. I decided I'd take my chances.

Eric and Kristen offered to lead us to Shepherd Lake, a beach in Ringwood State Park. I imagined it filled with families and giggling kids. He explained that visitors could rent boats, and there was even a concession stand.

From the lake, we headed to the Ringwood Manor. It was very stately. It was built in 1807 by Martin Ryerson. We started our tour at the original Ryerson entrance. If the staircase didn't convince you that these people were rich, the piazza did. It was a huge room, added in 1910, with large, floor-to-ceiling arched windows and filled with statues. For almost fifty years, Martin Reyerson, his wife, his three sons, and their families lived in the mansion. *Lucky people,* I thought.

Eventually, Abraham and Sarah Cooper Hewitt bought the property. Since Abraham's partner and father-in-law, Peter Cooper, stayed over often, we got to see his bedroom and writing desk. We learned that the dining room was the center of Ringwood Manor during Abraham Hewitt's political career. Here, so many dignitaries were entertained that Ringwood Manor came to be called the "Little White House." Meals often had 13-courses with a different wine served at each. Amazing, I thought, we're standing in what was once called the Little White House.

There were so many rooms. A music room had a giant mural of boats on the sea, and there was a North Ryerson Parlor and a South Ryerson Parlor. There was a nursery, a sewing room, a waiting room, a great hall, a drawing room, and many private bedrooms. Eric pointed out the many outbuildings, like the blacksmith and the laundry building. There were numerous items on display from various places in New York City. Eric told us that as the two giant eagle statues at the park entrance were from New York's Penn Station in Manhattan.

We met Mark and Cliff, two of the gardeners, and they were very happy to point out various flowers and plants. They did an amazing job, and I figured this had to be a very popular park.

We wondered how hard it must have been to be responsible for so many resources: thousands of acres, two enormous manors, the state botanical gardens, and the beach. We thanked them both and told them there would be a report on the website to make sure everyone in New Jersey knew how awesome these places were.

After the manors, we did some hiking. The views, as my grandfather repeated, were breathtaking. This was the same state that had big cities, rolling farmland, and dozens of beaches. It was pretty incredible. As we left, we noticed a small waterfall near the entrance and I decided, right then and there, that I would have a waterfall when I grew up. I could have listened to that water all day.

There must have been something in the mountain air, because it was the quietest ride home ever. At one point I turned around to see if T-Bone and Wanda were still in the car. As I turned, I could see his eyes were as big as half dollars and he had a smile frozen on his face. Just as I was about to ask him if he was dehydrated, I looked a little further and noticed the cause of his wildly crazy expression. Wanda had fallen asleep, and her head must have slid to the side and landed neatly on his shoulder.

I grabbed my notebook and, in giant letters, wrote, AWWW…HOW CUTE. I assumed he would be totally embarrassed and move her head back to her headrest.

Instead, he nodded and silently, slowly mouthed the words, "*I know.*"

Chapter Seven

The next morning was an actual Saturday with no day trip planned. It was hard to believe, but in a little more than a week, we had visited Wharton State Forest, Batsto Village, Atsion Recreation Area, Brendan T. Byrne State Forest, Whitesbog Village, Ringwood Manor State Park, and the State Botanical Gardens. I looked at my list of state parks, forests, recreation areas, and marinas and started checking off all the sites we had written a report about.

As I searched through my documents, I was surprised to see how many places we had visited and written about. There was our trip to High Point State Park and Stokes State Forest, one of our first *Garden State Adventures*. It was on that trip that we discovered Sunrise Mountain and Lake Marcia. Suddenly, I wanted to know more about their history. I knew High Point earned its name by being the highest point in New Jersey at 1,803 feet, and Sunrise Mountain seemed easy enough. But what about Stokes State Forest or Lake Marcia? I wondered if Kevin Woyce covered this in his book. As I opened his e-book once more, I stumbled upon the answers.

Apparently, Lake Marcia was named after the fiancée of a state geologist in 1855. I decided I better not share that with T-Bone. Knowing him, he'd become a geologist and spend his life searching for a lake to name after Wanda.

Next was Stokes State Forest, and I needed to know if there was a person named Stokes. If history was an indicator, it would be a man, and I remembered seeing a Stokes Elementary School in Trenton. That meant he was probably an important man. There it was. Edward Stokes was the governor of New Jersey from 1905-1908. He fought hard to limit the power of railroads and utility companies, he worked to improve education, and recommended that the state begin buying and preserving its dwindling forests. Yes, he was definitely an important man if you liked nature, clean air, and clean water.

In October 1905, the new Forest Park Reservation Commission made its first purchase, two tracts of land totaling 970 acres. A 1907 purchase, 5,432 acres in Sussex County, became the heart of Stokes State Forest. These woodlands were not parks like local parks, however. They weren't filled with swings, slides, and fountains. They were more natural, and visitors were welcome to hike, camp, hunt or fish.

I decided when T-Bone wrote his thank-you letter to Governor Byrne, I was sending one to Kevin Woyce. His book was so interesting it should be required reading for all kids and anyone visiting a park or forest. Knowing the history of a place we were visiting and about the people who created it made our trips much more interesting. If we were accepting applications for associate ambassadors, I'd definitely try to recruit Kevin Woyce, Governor Brendan Byrne, and, I guess, Wanda.

As I searched our files, I found several more state sites we had already visited and written about. There was Allaire State Park, complete with an historic 19th-century iron-making town. Inside the park was the Allaire Village, preserving the history of the village life at what was once called the Howell Iron Works, and the life of James Peter Allaire.

"Hey, what are you doing?" asked T-Bone as he walked through the family room with a large envelope.

"Tallying up how many state parks and forests we've visited," I replied. "Whatcha got there?"

"Wow, that must be some list," said T-Bone. "Did you get High Point and Stokes?"

"Yup," I nodded. "What's in the envelope?"

"How about Allaire State Park and the village?" he asked.

"Got it," I answered, momentarily forgetting about the envelope in his hand. "Oh wait, here's another one; remember Barnegat Lighthouse? That's a state park, too."

"Ol' Barney," T-Bone laughed, "how could I forget?"

"Not sure," I laughed. "It's been a while."

"You know what I liked best about that lighthouse?" he asked. "It was close to the water, and we could see the tip of Island Beach State Park. Plus, it was designed by General Meade from the Civil War."

"Okay, you do realize all lighthouses are near water, right?" I asked, hoping he knew the answer.

"Oops," he laughed, and covered his mouth just like Wanda did on our last trip. That was weird, I thought.

"And that's another good one. Island Beach is another state park that we've been to," I said.

"Ooh, don't forget the Delaware & Raritan Canal State Park, the state's seventy-mile linear park," he remembered.

"And one of, if not the best, bike paths in the state," I added. These parks were so great it was easy to get lost in the moment.

"Well, right across the street from the canal is Washington Crossing State Park," said T-Bone.

"I guess we know how it got its name, huh?" I laughed.

"How?" T-Bone stopped laughing and looked confused.

"Um, I'm pretty sure it earned the name by being the place

where General George Washington and his troops made their famous Delaware River Crossing on Christmas night," I said.

"Oh, it was named after the famous crossing?" he wondered out loud.

"Are you serious?" I asked.

"I like to consider myself lighthearted and carefree," he answered. "I'm hardly serious. Why?"

I told him to forget it. I learned a long time ago that it was sometimes pointless to keep explaining.

"We can't forget Ft. Mott," I mumbled. "Remember that was part of the coastal defense system. But why name it Mott? Who was Mott?"

"He was probably some kind of a soldier," T-Bone guessed.

"Why would you guess that?" I asked, very curious as to how he came up with that answer.

"I don't know," he shrugged, "probably because it was a military fort."

He was right. It was named after New Jersey resident and Civil War Brigadier General Gershon Mott. In fact, the fort was operated by the United States Army until 1943.

The state acquired the abandoned fort and turned it into a park in 1951.

"I've got one," I said, "remember Liberty State Park?"

"Do I remember?" he shrieked. "We arrived at the Liberty Science Center in a limo that I won for the day on the NJ 101.5 radio station contest."

"That was a great day," I agreed.

I remembered that visit well. Liberty State Park is the only place in New Jersey to offer ferry service to the Statue of Liberty and Ellis Island, and it has a backdrop different than every other state park. There are no mountains, rolling hills, or beaches; instead it's a panoramic view of the New York City skyline. That skyline gives this park the most unique setting of all New Jersey sites. And as amazing as the New York City skyline is, *you actually need to be in New Jersey to really appreciate it.*

"The battlefields are state parks," said T-Bone, "and we know how they got their names. There's the Monmouth Battlefield and Princeton Battlefield State Parks."

"True," I said, checking each place off of the list.

"How many kids do you think know about these great places or their history?" wondered T-Bone.

"Not enough," I answered, knowing we would have our

96

work cut out for us if we were going to make sure kids knew about and appreciated their state. We were also trying to encourage kids to get informed and then get involved in all levels of government, in that order. Every four years commercials encourage young voters to *rock the vote,* and while that's good, it's not enough. We needed to remind people to learn about the issues and have fact-based positions. Just showing up every four years is never good for the long term. I hoped we could get kids to see things differently; to understand that we have the same obligations that our founding fathers had. *We just had more conveniences and technology.*

After adding the new sites, the list of state parks and forests we visited and shared with other kids was pretty long. It was at that moment I remembered the large envelope in T-Bone's hand.

"What's in the envelope?" I reminded him.

"I have no idea," he shrugged as he set it on the table. "I just know that it's huge and it's heavy."

"How can you not know what's in it?" I asked
.

"I can't see through paper, can I?" he said, rolling his eyes.

"T-Bone, you walked in with that envelope," I said.

"Yes, but it's not mine," he shrugged his shoulders. "Your mailman handed it to me."

"Then why didn't you just say that?" I asked.

"Because, I believe, and correct me if I'm wrong," he said, sounding like a television detective, "that your question was *what's in the envelope* and I told you I didn't know."

I stared at him as I walked to the table and grabbed it, never once taking my eyes off of him. As I peeled back the tape and slid out the enormous stack of papers, I realized it was a package from our friend, Billy, at the State House. There was a note attached. As I pulled out the note, I could see T-Bone's face light up. Billy had received hundreds of emails and letters from kids all over the state. Some were sent to thank us, but most were sharing their favorite places in hopes we would visit them. He said he would forward the emails and wanted to send over the ones that came in the mail. I told T-Bone that Billy said he still hadn't heard anything about the Official Junior Ambassadors bills. T-Bone was crushed.

There were actual bills, basically the idea before it becomes a law or something official, to name us Official Junior Ambassadors. We simply needed one chamber of government to vote for us. It didn't have to be unanimous, and we didn't even need the governor's signature. We just needed half plus one to vote for us: twenty-one Senators or forty-one members of the General Assembly. We didn't understand what was taking so long. The title wouldn't affect how we were doing our job, but it would help us reach more kids, which would help New Jersey.

"How hard is it?" he gasped. "You say Nicky Fifth and T-Bone for Official Junior Ambassadors, and then you say all in favor."

"Maybe they're busy," I suggested.

"Of course they're busy," he said in a tone so serious it sounded grown-up. "But we're getting people in New Jersey excited about New Jersey. Doesn't that bring in money? *Isn't that important?*"

"Sure, but maybe there are more important things, or maybe we're next and we just don't know it," I said, ready to change the subject. "Anyway, we have a bunch of ideas from our fans, right here. That should make you happy."

"Yeah," he sighed. "It does."

We started reading them, and they were beyond good. They were great. We planned to read each and every one.

"This is my favorite part," I said, "besides visiting the places. It's fun to read about places other kids love."

"And there's so many here," said T-Bone. "There must be a thousand, and that doesn't count the emails."

"I know," I agreed. It was finally sinking in that kids, make that a lot of kids, were following our advice and our adventures. "Maybe we should take them over to the State House and let the legislators read them."

"Should we?" T-Bone shouted as he jumped up.

"No," I laughed, "I think we should read these letters."

I was happy whenever I found a letter about a place we had already visited. It confirmed that we had been doing a good job. Shawna Mellon, from Lincroft Elementary School, suggested the Grounds for Sculpture, one of our favorite places. Kristina Kerschner, from Memorial Elementary School in East Brunswick, wrote about the amazing and historic Old Barracks in Trenton. There were at least fifty letters for places like the boardwalk at Wildwood and the boardwalk at Seaside, Historic Cold Spring Village in Cape May, and Morristown.

T-Bone found all of the diner recommendations and held up two that sounded awesome. As the diner capital of the world, New Jersey had over 600 of these unique restaurants. We had become such huge fans of the Hibernia Diner in Rockaway, but we were always happy to visit a new one. Danny DiMarco, from Helen Morgan School in Sparta, wrote about the Jefferson Diner. T-Bone loved the idea of a great staff, delicious food, and lots of televisions. He even mentioned his teacher, Mrs. Feldman.

"Hold on," I said, "that name sounds familiar. There was a Mrs. Feldman at Alpine School in Sparta, and her students had excellent ideas. Think it's the same lady?"

"Probably," said T-Bone, "because there's a lot of good ones here, and there were a lot of good ones from the

Alpine School's Mrs. Feldman. And they're both in Sparta."

"They sure know their diners in North Jersey," I laughed.

"Uh-oh," said T-Bone as he waved a paper in the air. "Know what this is?"

"Nope."

"The Sparta Classic Diner," he gushed. "I love these kids. This is from Brandon Smith and he's from, drumroll please, Mrs. Feldman's class."

"Alpine School Mrs. Feldman or Helen Morgan School Mrs. Feldman?" I laughed.

We decided it was two sisters, a mother and a daughter, or the same lady in a different school. As we continued to sift through the piles, we came across so many great ideas. Samantha Dean, also from Mrs. Feldman's class, suggested Lake Mohawk with its stores, eateries, and boardwalk. Emily Guan, from Wayside Elementary School, told us about Joe Palaia Park, in Oakhurst, a relaxing park with a playground, a long hiking trail, and fireworks. Lily Albrecht, from Parkview School in Milltown, described The Milkway Pond and Waterfall in the Kittatinny Mountains. She even explained how she felt frost on her toes when she went in the waterfall.

"Awesome," I said. "We should tell people to go there."

"Forget that," T-Bone laughed, "*we should go there!*"

"Hold on," I said, as I waved a paper in the air. "Kelsi Loewen, from Mrs. Feldman's class, wrote about Boonton and the Boonton Waterfalls. She said both the town and the waterfall have interesting histories, and we should visit them both."

"Who knew we'd have so many waterfalls in New Jersey?" laughed T-Bone.

"I would," said my dad, as he walked into the family room. "You know the Paterson Falls, in Paterson, New Jersey, are the second largest falls on the East Coast, right?"

"Second?" asked T-Bone. "Who's first?"

"Just a little waterfall you may have heard of," said my dad, "called Niagara Falls."

"Are they real?" asked T-Bone.

"What?" my dad and I said at the same time.

"Are they real, or did I just see them on a show?" he asked.

"Both," said my dad.

"They had to be fake," T-Bone insisted. "They had colored lights, and a guy walked across on a tightrope. It must have been a movie."

"Tommy," my dad shook his head, "they're real. They're located between New York and Canada; there's the Horseshoe Falls and the American Falls. They light them up at night and a man did walk across, in real life."

"What?" T-Bone gasped, "I watched that whole thing. That was real? That wasn't a movie?"

My dad took a breath and explained that Nic Walenda, a famous tightrope walker from a famous tightrope family, walked across the tightrope, above the falls.

"That's unbelievable," he said, shaking his head. "Hey, wait a minute. Was the guy walking across a tightrope over the Grand Canyon real or a movie?"

"Same guy," I laughed. "But think about it, on the East Coast, our falls in Paterson are the next tallest after the world-famous Niagara Falls."

I came across a stack of letters from Lincroft Elementary School, and they had some great ideas. Logan Wyman wrote about tubing on the Delaware, and we came across students from all over the state who did the same. There were Alexander Blaszak and Margaret Piwko, from the Helen Morgan School, Sigal Gonzalez Hiatky from Ocean Township School, and Kitty Maas from Folwell School in Mount Holly. Every suggestion was great. Doug Fowler, from the Helen Morgan School, wrote about Thomas Edison's Lab in Menlo Park. Having visited the lab in West Orange, this was definitely a place we'd love to visit.

From Lincroft, Scott Toohey wrote about Thompson Park, Ian Rahill wrote about the Pine Barrens, Olivia Gandolfo wrote about Historic Smithville, and Mackenzie Montana and Sophia Romano wrote about a place called Poricy Park. We were so impressed with everyone's letters. Alana Spitzers, from Harrison School in Livingston, wrote about Chatham on pink paper and spoke about the history and the swamp. We remembered Mrs.Orozco from other students in her class who sent us letters.

Even though we were completely exhausted, we carefully went through every letter and email. When my mom called us for dinner, we couldn't believe the whole day had flown by so quickly. My dad suggested we pick three places and plan day trips. It sounded easy enough, but they were all so good.

Finally, we had made our decision. Jolene Gianone, from Lincroft School, also wrote about Poricy Park in Monmouth County, and her title immediately grabbed T-Bone's attention. It said, *Come back in time to the 1700s!* T-Bone's been waiting for an invitation to travel in time and the more he read, the more he was convinced that we should check out this park. Her descriptions of the activities and the farmhouse were very detailed, and we added Poricy Park to our list.

Next, Meira Davidowitz, from Ocean Township, also wrote about Historic Smithville. She guaranteed we would have a great time, and that was an offer we couldn't refuse. I was looking forward to the paddleboats.

But the letter that stood out the most was about Cheesequake State Park. It came in a homemade booklet with great pictures and was outstanding. Sarah Cassidy, from Lincroft School, painted such a vivid picture, I almost felt like I was in the park.

"Wow, her teacher must have really stressed painting pictures with your words," said T-Bone. "Although, I'm not sure if I like the idea of a fuzzy animal lurking about."

"Relax," I laughed, as I added Cheesequake State Park to the list. "She said fuzzy, not vicious. Plus, they have a lake and a beach."

I was remembering our trip to High Point and Lake Marcia again and hoping this would be similar. While it would be too cold to swim in October, we could definitely check it out and write a report. It was nine o'clock when we put our newly organized letters in a box. Knowing so many kids and their families appreciated what we were doing made our job awesome.

"You know, T-Bone," I started, "with all of these fans, it really doesn't matter if the state lawmakers make us Official Junior Ambassadors. I could live with being unofficial."

And with that, T-Bone stood up, slipped on his shoes, and headed to the door. As he opened the door, he stopped, turned his head, gave it some thought, and said, *"Speak for yourself, Nick. Speak for yourself."*

Chapter Eight

The next afternoon, I decided to watch some Sunday football with my dad. When I lived in Philly, we always cheered for the Eagles, but now I was torn. New Jersey didn't have a team, but they may as well have had one, since two New York teams played here. Even though they were both New York teams, the Giants and the Jets played at the Meadowlands. I really wasn't sure who I should root for, and living in New Jersey didn't make that choice easy. Most people who lived in south Jersey were Eagles fans, and North Jersey was filled with Giants and Jets fans.

Just as the game was about to kick off, the front door opened and in walked T-Bone.

"Whatcha doin'?" he asked.

"Watching ballet," I answered sarcastically.

"You sure?" he asked. "That looks like football to me."

"I'm sure," I said without turning my head. "It's definitely ballet."

"Hmmm," he mumbled as he grabbed the envelope from yesterday. "I'm going to look through these again."

T-Bone wasn't a huge sports fan. He liked politics, debates, and New Jersey more than anything. He was still determined to one day be governor, and one day be inducted into the New Jersey Hall of Fame. As the game got underway, he yelled, "Nick, Nick, did you see this?"

"See what?" I asked.

"A bunch of kids wrote about the place you're watching," he said.

"The place I'm watching?"

"Look, I thought I saw these yesterday," he explained. "This is exciting. Christian Ard, Brendan Antonelli, Michael Keenan, and Luke Mamola, all from Lincroft, wrote about the Metlife Stadium. So did Daniel Alves from Livingston."

"That's cool," I said. "I've never been there, but it looks awesome."

"Not only is it awesome," he continued, "did you know the 2014 Super Series will be played there. That's gonna be some match."

My dad and I just looked at each other. Only T-Bone could combine football, baseball, and tennis. But he was right:

on February 2, 2014, Super Bowl XLVIII would be huge for New Jersey. My dad and I were surprised when they picked Metlife Stadium. We weren't shocked because of the actual stadium, but because of the weather. February in New Jersey is usually pretty cold and snowy. Most Super Bowls that I remembered were in warm states or stadiums with domes. Without a warm winter or a dome, my dad said this championship would be *old school*. He told us about some famous games played in near blizzards.

"The new stadium is technologically superior and more earth-friendly than the old stadium," said T-Bone.

My dad grabbed a handful of chips and laughed. "It would be weird if it wasn't, right?"

"Oops, I guess so," said T-Bone as he covered his mouth like Wanda again. "Hey, Nick, maybe we should write a report about how exciting it is for New Jersey to host the Soup Bowl."

"Okay," I sighed. "It's a Super Bowl, and yes, we should definitely make sure kids know what an honor this is."

During halftime, T-Bone took out his mom's tablet. We decided to browse the Pocket Ranger app and select the next few sites we would visit. Soon, we came up with our next fabulous destinations. We selected Allamuchy Mountain State Park and Swartswood State Park. Eventually, we would visit Double Trouble, Hacklebarney, and Jenny Jump State Parks. There was no rhyme or reason for our choices; the truth is that every New Jersey park or forest was amazing. Rather than select randomly, we decided to use different criteria. We picked them based on their unusual names.

I used to tease my mom for picking sports teams based on their names or their colors, and here I was picking Hacklebarney because I couldn't think of anything funnier than Hacklebarney. Now, I just hoped our assistant would agree with our choices. And I really hoped Kevin Woyce wrote about these sites, too.

We arranged for my grandfather to bring us to Allamuchy Mountain State Park the following Saturday. That gave us time to get our schoolwork done and prepare for the trip. Starting Monday, Wanda and T-Bone stayed after school trying to start the programs they campaigned on, and I stuck around to help them. We worked with the teachers making invitations for senior citizens to volunteer at the school, and the response was overwhelming. Who would have thought so many people would be eager to go back to middle school? We also started planning a school garden. The PTA believed in the idea so much they donated the money for a small greenhouse. Our agriscience teachers taught us how to germinate seeds and plan a garden. It was only October, but successful gardens required serious planning. I hated to admit it, but T-Bone and Wanda really made a good team.

Saturday morning, when my grandfather arrived, Wanda and I were sitting in the kitchen.

"Where's Tommy?" he asked.

"Don't know," I shrugged. "This has never happened before."

It was true. I couldn't remember the last time I walked downstairs and T-Bone wasn't sitting there. Just as I was about to call him, I heard him come flying through the front door.

"I'm here, I'm here!" he yelled, waking up the whole house. "Don't leave, I'm here. Nick! Nick!"

As he ran into the kitchen and realized we hadn't left without him, he hit the brakes. It was too late. His momentum got the best of him and he slid into the kitchen cabinets. Everyone stood speechless. By the time he rolled over to get up, my parents, my sisters, and my brother were also standing in the kitchen.

"I'm okay, I'm okay," he said as he stood up and dusted himself off. He was wearing the white outfit and orange hat again. I quickly turned to look at my dad.

"What's he supposed to be?" he asked my mom.

"Shhh! Don't be rude," she reprimanded.

"*But he looks like a bottle of glue,*" my dad said as he rubbed his head and went back upstairs.

"I know, dear," my mom nodded. "I know."

Once the excitement ended, we started our journey to Allamuchy Mountain State Park. Wanda was ready to dazzle us with some facts. I was hoping she had the origin of the name.

"So, I used Kevin Woyce's book and found out why it's called Allamuchy Mountain," she began. "Long story short, the name has been used since 1715 when a surveyor named Reading was working for William Penn."

"He should have lived in Pennsylvania," said T-Bone.

"He founded Pennsylvania," I said, speaking on behalf of my home state. "And no, it was not a coincidence that it was named Pennsylvania; it was named *after* him."

"Well," Wanda continued, "he was exploring the Pequest River, a twenty-five mile tributary of the Delaware River when he told Penn about a village with the name Allamucha. It was the shortened version of a Lenape Indian chief's name and meant *place with the hills*. Much of the land used for this park came from the Rutherfurd and Stuyvesant estates. These families are the direct descendants of Peter Stuyvesant, the last governor of New Amsterdam, now New York."

"How big is it?" I asked.

"8,893 acres," she replied. "If you like fishing, the

Musconectong River winds through the park and offers some of the best trout fishing in the state. They also have hiking and biking trails, a canoe launch, horseback riding trails, and a scenic overlook."

"What's the history?" asked T-Bone, in an all-business voice.

"You're not going to get mad when I tell you, are you?" she asked him.

"Oh, no," he put his head in his hands, "what did they knock down? What irreplaceable piece of history is lost forever?"

"Wow," she said as she looked at me. "You weren't kidding; *he is a mess*."

I had already warned Wanda that T-Bone never handled lost history well. Hopefully, she wasn't about to tell him about a mansion that was knocked down.

"Okay, it's not that bad," she started. "You see, there was this really awesome restoration of Andover Forge, which was also a port on the very busy Morris Canal, called Waterloo Village. Some of the buildings and structures located in the historic district are on the New Jersey and National Register of Historic Places."

"But?" T-Bone asked slowly.

"But," she continued, "the village was run by a private foundation for many years. Since January 1, 2007, the state has managed the site. The park was open, but there were no programs or costumed interpreters."

"Well, that's not good," said T-Bone.

"Okay, before you start writing letters to Trenton," Wanda began, "several groups have supported the Village like the Canal Society of New Jersey, Friends of Waterloo Village, and the Winakung at Waterloo."

"Is the Village still there?" he asked.

Wanda nodded.

"And the buildings haven't been torn down?" he asked.

Wanda nodded.

"And we can go in them?" he tried once more.

Wanda shook her head.

"See, Nick, that's what I mean," T-Bone exclaimed, "why doesn't anyone care?"

"People do care," she smiled at T-Bone in a way I had never seen before. "Don't forget, they didn't tear it down, did they?"

"Yet," he said. "Yet. There's probably a demolition order on some person's desk just waiting to be signed, and I bet all the people ordering the demolition have never even been here. They probably don't appreciate what, I'm sure, is awesome history. I bet they don't realize how good these places are for education and the local economy. Why you, Waterloo? Why you?"

"Are you done?" asked Wanda. "The state has actually been investing money, and those organizations have been working hard to restore it. The Canal Society hosts ten Canal Days between June and October, and the Friends and Winakung groups have created amazing field trips for schools. I spoke with a woman named Andrea Proctor who is the resource interprative specialist and she'll answer our questions."

We parked and headed toward the building where Andrea would meet us. There was a white church nearby, and it looked like it was still in use. The building was cool and really huge. It had a giant fireplace, one right behind it, then another on the other side of the enormous room.

"Good morning, I'm Andrea Proctor," a woman said as she approached. "I believe we spoke on the phone."

"Yes, we did," Wanda confirmed. "We actually have a lot of questions for you. I hope that's okay."

"Of course," she smiled. "That's why I'm here."

"Well, I did some research and I was hoping you could give me the history of the village," Wanda said as she opened up her notebook.

"And I'd like a present," said T-Bone, on the verge of becoming flustered.

"Excuse me?" Andrea asked. "Did you say you want a present, *as in a gift?*"

"Do you give away gifts, like T-shirts?" he asked. "Because, if you do, I'd like a large; you know how cotton shrinks."

Andrea looked confused, and Wanda looked like she was about to lose her patience.

"No, she is not giving away gifts," Wanda said to T-Bone, then turned to Andrea, "and no, he meant he wants to know what's happening with the village *in the present.*"

Andrea looked relieved and decided to address the past first. She said if she were the Allamuchy Mountains and had been watching the village, she would have seen the Lenni Lenape, the original inhabitants, followed by the Europeans. The Lenape became ill from diseases the Europeans brought with them. There were conflicts, and the Europeans often took advantage of them. The Lenape eventually moved to Pennsylvania, then Ohio, and then they separated.

The iron ore era was next, as the trees and rocks made farming difficult. To fuel the blast furnace, trees were turned into charcoal and eventually the trees were gone.

"You don't mean all of the trees, do you?" asked T-Bone, suddenly in a panic.

"Pretty much," she said. "But the next era, after the advances in iron production and without trees to provide charcoal, was the farming era."

"That kind of makes sense," I agreed.

"Well, if I were those mountains," she continued, "the next thing I'd see would be the canal era. The Morris Canal was vital for transporting goods."

"We're actually canal fans," said T-Bone. "We're big fans of the Delaware & Raritan Canal."

"Then you inderstand how important they are," she said with a smile. "That's wonderful. Not many kids appreciate the past like you kids."

"Thank you," I said. "But did trains really put this canal out of business?"

"Well, just like something better and more economical put the iron ore furnaces out of business, trains were faster and more efficient," she explained.

Just then, two women walked in the door. It was two of the costumed interpreters, Marie Kovacs and Susan Wojcik. Marie portrayed Mrs. Miller from the gristmill, while Susan portrayed the wealthy Mrs. Smith.

"Who was Mrs. Smith?" I asked.

"That's a good question," said Susan. "In 1815, General John Smith purchased this tract of land. The General never lived here; he actually bought it because of its location next to the river and canal and also for the opportunities they brought."

"It was his sons that lived here," said Marie. Peter and his wife had eleven children and a few of their sons were very active with the village. Samuel, Seymour and Peter Decker were all residents. Ironically, their large, exquisite homes were right next to multi-family tenant homes."

"Can we see them?" asked Wanda.

"Absolutely," said Andrea as we headed toward the door.

The leaves were every fall color you could imagine, and the air was crisp. We walked behind the church, and Andrea told us that the church was still active. Our first stop was the General Store, built in 1831 and right up against the canal. There were baskets hanging, kitchen supplies, food, and miniature furniture.

"Hey, they sold doll house furniture?" T-Bone laughed.

"No," Andrea smiled, "these are small samples of what people could order."

"Oh, I get it," he nodded. "The stove would be bigger?"

"I sure hope so," said my grandfather. "It would be hard to feed a family on a twelve-inch stove."

There was an old-fashioned washing machine, complete with rollers and an enormous coffee grinder. The strangest thing was the post office at the front of the store. They told us Seymour was the postmaster. I looked out the window and pictured a mule towing a boat along the canal. It must have been exciting for kids when the boats arrived.

Marie held up a bar of Ivory Soap and asked us what was so special about it. My grandfather couldn't help himself and immediately blurted out, "Ivory soap floats."

He was right; losing your bar of soap while bathing in a canal or river could be expensive. When people realized Ivory soap floated, it became very popular.

Next, Andrea handed us character cards that told us what we needed to look for. T-Bone's was great. He was a muskrat hunter and learned that the muskrats created a real problem. They created holes in the tow path, and mules could break their leg if they stepped in one. That could cause a significant problem for everyone and could be very expensive. Muskrat hunters provided a valuable service.

It only took T-Bone a few seconds to locate the snowshoes and lunch pail listed on his card. Unfortunately, it took me over five minutes to find the rug beater. I never thought about it, but without vacuum cleaners, rug beaters were the only way to beat dirt out of carpets.

We walked through the village and visited the gristmill, the blacksmith, and the canal museum. Andrea spoke to us as if we were a school tour, and I decided I would beg my school to take us on the full tour.

Some of the houses were under construction, and we asked when the work would be done. Sadly, the work is very slow. Throughout New Jersey, there are so many homes and historic sites that need renovations and maintenance and state funds are limited.

"I have an idea," said T-Bone. "What if we tell kids about these buildings?"

"And then what?" I said. "Kids don't have a lot of money."

"What if every school adopted one historic site?" he said with a giant grin and a wild nod.

I hated to admit it, but T-Bone was on to something. If each school pulled their resources and adopted one site, New Jersey's past would really be protected. Plus, kids would become experts on their sites.

Andrea, Susan, and Marie thought it was a fabulous way to learn and give back while doing something positive. *T-Bone did it again.*

When we were about to leave, Andrea told us about the Lenape Winakung village and we were excited to see it.

It was so much more than I expected. It was like walking into a Native American village. There was the Longhouse, which was like a dorm. Several family members would live in this twenty feet wide by sixty feet long shelter. There was a shelf around the lower part of the longhouse and that's where family members slept; the shelf above that was for storage. There was a family of manequins, in costume, demonstrating what a family would do inside. Throughout the Lenape village there were several exhibits with manequins and items that made it seem very real.

There was a hunting exhibit, as well as gardening, skins, pottery, cooking, medicine, relationships, and ceremonies. For the first time, I understood what it was like to be a Native American. Their connection with the earth was so important. My favorite fact was the *Guardian of the Garden*. A child would often stand guard over the garden to prevent animals from destroying their crops. At first, it sounded funny, until Andrea reminded us that lost or destroyed food could not be replaced at a supermarket.

"I think every kid should see this," said T-Bone. "But which tour would you recommend? The village and the Lenni Lenape tours are both great."

"Good news," exclaimed Andrea. "Schools can pick one or choose shorter versions of both."

"That's awesome," said Wanda. "I think the next report should introduce kids to your adopt-a-site idea and field trips. I think if more teachers knew what Waterloo Village had to offer, even more schools would come."

"You should also keep an eye on the Morris Canal Greenway," Andrea suggested. "It will connect a walking path that runs across the whole state."

"No way," said T-Bone. "We could walk east to west?"

"Or we could walk west to east," I added, not sure if he realized it wouldn't be a one-way path.

"Keep in contact with state lawmakers and let them know you think it's important," my grandfather added.

I was so happy we visited the village and got to meet the ladies. As we were leaving, Marie pulled me aside and told me why Andrea was so knowledgeable and excited. It turned out she was the founder of Winakung at Waterloo. She loved the village since her childhood and worked there when the private foundation was running it. When the foundation lost its lease she knew that the programs would end. But, Andrea said one simple sentence: *"There's got to be something we can do."* And she did it. She founded Winakung at Waterloo, a non-profit organization that would help coordinate school programs.

"You know, kids," said my grandfather, "what Andrea did, what the Canal Society, the Friends of Waterloo, and every other civic group does is so important. They fill in the gaps and protect resources. They're great examples."

"You know what's missing from many of these groups?" asked Andrea. When no one answered, she told us. "Kids and young adults are missing. If we don't start getting younger people involved, eventually the civic groups that save everything won't be able to save themselves."

I had never thought about that, but she was right. This was important and would have to be in the next report. I hoped Wanda was taking really good notes.

As we started to thank everyone, two gentlemen walked over. We were introduced to Steve Ellis, the acting regional superintendent for the northern region and Mark Texel, the director of state park services.

When we told them what we were doing, they thought exploring state parks and forests was a great idea. We told them that we'd like to encourage schools and classes to adopt buildings, and they thought that could really help.

"So, what's next?" asked Steve.

"Allamuchy Mountain State Park," T-Bone grinned.

"You'll get two state parks for the price of one," he said. "Stephen's State Park is adjacent to Allamuchy."

"Is it far?" asked T-Bone.

"Adjacent means attached," said my grandfather.

"Allamuchy is less developed with more passive offerings, like hiking and bird-watching," he said. "Stephens has camping, hunting, fishing, rock climbing, boating, picnicking, and an interpretive nature center."

"And you're sure they're definitely connected?" asked T-Bone. "Because that would make it easy."

"We're positive," Steve said with a smile. We shook their hands and thanked them for speaking with us; and also for protecting New Jersey.

"So who was Stephens?" I asked, wondering how much research Wanda had really done.

"Well, Stephens Park is considerably smaller than Allamuchy Mountain at 805 acres. The last 238 acres were donated by Marsena P. and Augustus W. Stephens."

We started at Allamuchy and did a little hiking. There were harder trails on one side of the park and easy-to-moderate trails on the other side. The air was cool enough so we didn't start sweating as we hiked. Along the way, T-Bone stopped and spoke with anyone who wasn't smart enough to keep walking. We met some very nice people, and an older couple suggested we drive by the Big House. I thought they meant prison, but Wanda knew better.

They were referring to Rutherfurd Hall, known by the family as the Big House. It was also adjacent to Allamuchy State Park. They told us it was a work in progress and a beautiful estate. We decided to drive by.

The whole area was gorgeous, and the fall leaves made the background even nicer. I decided I also wanted to see these parks in the winter when they were snow-covered.

We drove past Rutherfurd Hall, and it looked like a castle. It was huge, with a school in the front building. Some very dedicated groups of people had been working hard to restore the hall and preserve the history. How lucky were the people who lived in this castle along a mountainous state park? I started daydreaming that I lived there. We soon left and headed to Stephens State Park.

It seemed like there were more people at Stephens Park than Allamuchy Park. We saw everything from families with strollers and dogs taking leisurely walks to serious hikers on a mission. We sat along the Musconectong River, and it sounded as awesome as it looked. I noticed a few people fishing and realized how peaceful these parks were. They were more than a natural resource and valuable history, they were a place to relax and unwind, a place to spend time with family and friends, and a place to get exercise. Those benefits alone were enough to make these parks a priority.

On the way home, my grandfather pulled off of Route 80 and I recognized the exit immediately. We were heading to the Hibernia Diner, and I couldn't have been happier. We did a lot of exploring and definitely worked up an appetite. And now, I'd be able to give Wanda some information. As I told her about our friend, George, who was the owner, he came walking up to our table. "There they are!" he exclaimed. "New Jersey's Official Junior Ambassadors. How are you guys?"

"Not official yet," I said with a shrug.

"What's taking them so long?" he said with a smile. "*Do you want me to call Trenton?*"

"Yes," said T-Bone. "Can you call them now?"

"He's not really calling them," I whispered. "He's joking."

"Okay, what would help you feel better today?" he asked. "Pie? Ice cream?"

"Yes and yes," said T-Bone.

"Four a la mode pies coming right after your meals," he announced as he headed toward the kitchen.

It was great seeing George and eating at the Hibernia. I was very proud to live in the *Diner Capital of the World*. Diners were like second homes. You could have meatloaf, a turkey dinner, seafood, or scrambled eggs, any time of the day. And when you walked into a diner, you felt welcome. Even *difficult Wanda* enjoyed herself.

As we drove home, I couldn't wait to go to bed. Wanda agreed to write the report, and that was just fine with me. She had been taking all of the notes anyway, so it made more sense. Plus, I was exhausted. I really didn't know where she found the energy.

"So," T-Bone began as we neared our town. "Anyone have plans tomorrow?"

I was afraid to hear his idea and more afraid that it would require me to wake up early. I was right. "I was thinking we should shoot down to Historic Smithville," he said. "Remember, Meira Davidowitz guaranteed we'd love it?"

"I'm busy, but your dad is off," said my grandfather.

"Great, we'll ask him," said T-Bone.

My dad must have been in a strange mood when we returned home. As soon as T-Bone suggested it, he agreed. It happened so fast I couldn't stop it. Now, I'd have to get up early on the one day I could possibly sleep in.

"Good news, Nick," said T-Bone as he walked by. "Your dad is in. See you bright and early!"

"Yeah," I nodded, "thanks."

"Don't mention it," he winked.

Chapter Nine

As soon as I placed my head on my pillow, the alarm went off. At least it seemed that way. And by alarm, I meant T-Bone knocking at the door way earlier than he needed to be over at my house. In the old days, my mom would run down the hall so my brother, Timmy, and my sisters, Emma and Maggie, wouldn't wake up. Now, they all yelled, "Nicky, go get that," from their rooms.

I let T-Bone and Wanda in and reminded them that they were a little early. They knew. It took an hour for my whole family to get ready. I counted eight people and was just about to volunteer to stay home and sleep. Then I remembered our new van had eight seats. I had to face it; I was not going back to sleep anytime soon.

Historic Smithville was located in Galloway Township, not far from Atlantic City and the Atlantic Ocean. We were visiting the Towne of Historic Smithville and the Village Greene. It was centered on Lake Meone and had forty shops and numerous restaurants. The first thing I noticed was the train that Meira wrote about. As soon as my sisters saw it, they wanted a ride. That whining lasted until they saw the carousel. That crying only lasted until they saw the paddleboats. If they would have spotted the candy store, it would have been game over. My mom told them we were eating lunch before we did anything.

We walked by the Historic Smithville Inn, and it looked very historic and fancy. It was definitely not the place to bring my two sisters, who were in the car for an hour and were already crying about a train and a carousel. My mom noticed a place called AJ's on the Lake, and it looked perfect. We could eat outside with the two cranky girls and even better, they served breakfast all day long. Maggie and Emma shared pancakes, my mom got a salad, my dad got chili, and T-Bone, Timmy, Wanda, and I all ordered burgers. It was delicious, and I loved eating outside across from the lake. If I could have, I'd have moved our kitchen table to the backyard.

"So where should we go first?" asked T-Bone as we finished our lunch. This was a big mistake from a kid with no younger brothers and sisters. He didn't know about *choices*. Being the oldest kid, my mom taught me about choices when my brother was born. She always said that you never ask a child what they want to do. You never ask them what they want to eat or what they want to wear. Instead, you ask them if they would like carrots or broccoli? Would they like to wear the blue dress or the red dress? But, never, ever, under any circumstances, should you ask a kid an open question.

As soon as T-Bone asked the question, everyone yelled a different answer. The girls wanted to go on the carousel,

Timmy and Wanda wanted to go on the paddleboats, my mom said shopping, and my dad said the tavern. We all knew he wanted to find a television somewhere and watch a football game.

Unfortunately, for everyone else, cranky little kids usually get first choice. Today was no exception. We headed to the carousel, and we all waved as they whirled by. Lap after lap, we waved every single time. Six people wildly waving at two little girls who pretended they didn't know us. *Looking back, I couldn't blame them.*

Our next stop was the train, and my mom insisted we all take a ride. It was decorated for Halloween, and my sisters and T-Bone were really excited. It was a beautiful fall day, but it was also the kind of day that reminded you winter wasn't far off. Soon sweatshirts and baseball caps would be replaced with big coats, mittens, and winter hats. Casually strolling would be replaced with quick steps and chattering teeth. I decided to savor every moment, even if that included a Halloween train ride.

When it was time for the paddleboats on the lake, my mom and my sisters made a quick getaway. From the moment we arrived, I could see her eyeballing the stores. I knew her so well, I knew exactly where she would go.

She would start at the candle shop, then stop in the Christmas shop, the cook's store, the Irish store, and several gift shops. If my sisters got fussy, she would pop in the candy store to buy herself some time. I could also guarantee that if she bought anything, she would quietly go to the car. This is where she would pretend to get juice bags and hide whatever she bought. As we paddled through the center of the village, I was the only one paying attention to her. I found her routines amusing. I could see her going in those stores, one by one, almost in the exact order I predicted. Then I observed her, bags in hand, heading to the car. When she returned, there were no more shopping bags, but Maggie and Emma had juice bags.

The weather was so nice, my dad sprung for all of us to ride the boats twice. I was shocked because the ride was thirty minutes, and three people fit in a boat. For the first ride, my dad and my brother were in one boat and T-Bone, Wanda, and I were in the other. When we got out and my dad suggested we go again, T-Bone started giving me a weird look.

"What's wrong?" I asked.

He didn't answer; he just strained his face harder. His eyebrows were furrowed, and he was wide-eyed. His stare was so intense, it was like he was trying to send me a telepathic message.

"What?" I asked, partly exasperated and partly confused.

When Wanda wasn't looking, he started pointing his head toward her. I shook my head. I had no idea what he was trying to say and why he couldn't speak. By this point, everyone, including Wanda, was looking at him.

"Does he need a doctor?" asked Timmy. "He's got sweat dripping by his eye, and it's not even hot out."

"Nick, do something about that," said my dad, pointing at T-Bone's head and walking over to pay for the next rides.

I was just about to pull him aside when my mom walked over with the girls. She told my dad to get a third boat for them and surprisingly, he didn't faint. *I wondered if we had secretly hit the lottery.* My mom quickly glanced in T-Bone's direction, immediately understood what he wanted, and told me and my brother to ride with my dad. I finally got it. The next question, however, was how my mom figured out that T-Bone wanted to ride alone with Wanda. No one else could make heads or tails of his crazy charades. My mom walked up, casually glanced, and solved the puzzle. *Another mysterious mom thing.*

As we loaded the boats, T-Bone came very close to getting his wish. Everyone was lined up in the exact order necessary to make his dream come true. My mom and the girls were together, my dad and my brother stood with me, and T-Bone stood with Wanda. It was all set. He would have thirty glorious minutes alone with Wanda on a paddle -boat. Of course, from Wanda's perspective, you could say she would be trapped on a boat with T-Bone for a long half hour. T-Bone couldn't have been happier. He stood there with that big goofy grin on his face, probably practicing poetry in his head. They looked like Alfalfa and Darla from *The Little Rascals*.

Then, at the very last second, Wanda told my mom she would ride with the girls so my parents could have a romantic ride without kids. T-Bone's face dropped as my parents stepped into the boat. Knowing what just happened, my dad put his arm around my mom and waved at T-Bone. He was crushed. As Wanda and my little sisters stepped into the next boat, I could see him scrambling to come up with a new configuration. It was useless. There were six people left and two boats. No matter how he arranged everyone, there would have to be three people in each boat. As Timmy and I joined him, he realized he would not get to ride with Wanda *at all*.

"Well, on the bright side," I said, pointing to my parents, "at least someone's having a romantic ride."

He wasn't amused. When we finally stopped paddling, my parents treated us to ice cream. We walked through the Village and the Greene, thoroughly decorated with pumpkins and fall decorations. My mom even managed to stop in a few more stores. Soon, everyone was hungry for dinner and surprisingly, my dad headed toward the Historic Smithville Inn. This restaurant dated back to 1787 and was voted Best Off-Shore Restaurant. When my dad saw the long line, he turned around. Two things he hated were spending money and waiting in line, and I knew he wouldn't do both. We headed to Fred and Ethel's Lantern Light Tavern. The atmosphere was fun and more casual, probably the best choice for my sisters. They had a large selection and a kids' menu. Even better, the menu included the history of Smithville and the history of Fred and Ethel. We read every word. At first, Wanda thought they were the characters from her favorite television show, *I Love Lucy*. This, however, was an *actual coincidence*.

According to the menu, the town of Smithville thrived until the days of the railroad, which changed everything. Stagecoach usage dwindled and vanished, and Smithville found itself a small and lonely place. The Inn fell into a state of disrepair, which is how Fred and Ethel Noyes discovered the property in 1949. Fred Winslow Noyes, Jr. and Ethel Marie Noyes, both lovers of southern New Jersey history, looked past the Inn's decay and saw immense potential. Together they formed a vision and realized a dream: bringing the past to life through the Historic Towne of Smithville.

They collected historically significant, original structures from throughout the region, bringing them to Smithville and restoring them to their former beauty. The Historic Towne of Smithville opened in the early 1950s, welcoming visitors from all over the world. Articles in prominent publications such as the *New York Times* praised the Towne's unique charm and beauty.

Fred and Ethel's love of history and hospitality inspired the present owners, Laura and Chuck Bushar and Fran and Tony Coppola, to recreate the spirit of the old Lantern Light Inn. It said, *As you enjoy your meal, think of the many travelers and the feasts they enjoyed centuries ago over tall tales of all sorts. Stroll through the Towne, and you'll catch a glimpse of those fascinating bygone days.*

"They're my kind of people," said T-Bone, "they love history and hospitality. And it reminds me of Cold Spring Village in Cape May. Remember how they collected authentic buildings and created an historic village?"

"You're right," I agreed. "I always think about all of the travelers who must have eaten at the places we visit. Sometimes, when I enter an historic building, I wonder how many people walked through that specific doorway or sat by that specific fireplace. Then I wonder who they were and if they were famous."

"Do you wonder what they discussed?" asked T-Bone.

"Definitely," I nodded.

"You know what's cool," said Wanda. "Look at their early history. They were so popular when travel by sea was popular. Then, trains came and Smithville was forgotten."

"That's not cool," said T-Bone. "It's the opposite of cool."

"No, not the being forgotten part," she said, shaking her head. "I'm talking about where they are today. They re-invented themselves. They utilized their assets, their history, their location near the ocean, and the things that make them unique."

"That's kind of like Trenton, right?" I asked my dad. "Pop says they have the potential for a complete renaissance."

"It's very similar," my dad agreed. "During Trenton's best years, it was a leader in manufacturing. Once automation made manufacturing easier and companies moved their production to foreign countries, the city lost valuable jobs. Once a downward spiral starts, it can become difficult to reverse it."

"Do you think Trenton can re-invent itself, Mr. A.?" asked T-Bone.

"Sure," said my dad. "Steady, solid leadership that uses the city's history and riverfront location can attract investors and state support. Remember, it's our capital. We need all of our cities to succeed, especially our capital. It's a matter of pride and reflects on everyone."

"Why don't you run for office, Mr. A.?" asked T-Bone.

"Well, Tommy," he said, "I have all the faith in the world in our system of government, but not as much in some of the people we trust to run our government. I feel like during a campaign, they're all smiles and ready to shake your hand and listen to your concerns or ideas. After the campaign, you can't find them anywhere."

"Actually, Mr. A.," said Wanda, "I agree, we have a representative form of government and serving as an elected official was supposed to be a duty, not a career. But if someone wants to keep getting elected, they need a lot of money, and to get a lot of donations, they have to make a lot of promises, and then guess what?"

135

"Ooh, I know," said T-Bone, "they work day and night to fulfill every promise."

"Wrong," Wanda continued, "they start responding more to those who can contribute money, *a lot of money*. Money in politics and career politicians have made it hard for average people to have a real voice."

"Wow," said my mom, "and I thought my husband had strong views. Is that what your parents told you?"

"No, Mrs. A.," she said, "I watch of a lot of different channels and read a lot of articles. I only comment if I know enough about the topic."

"Wow," my mom repeated. "Adults could take a lesson from your book. Now I see why you three kids get along so well."

The Lantern Light smelled so good, I knew the food would be awesome. My sisters spent most of the meal coloring while the rest of us talked politics. By the time our meal was finished, we had solved all of the world's problems, or at least most of them. Together, we decided to limit campaign donations, limit the campaign season, and limit the number of times you can get elected. It sounded so reasonable; I couldn't understand why no one would change it.

My dad told us that in order for it to change, those who benefit from all of the problems would have to the fix them. He said that was unlikely. It seemed so hopeless. Then he said the electorate, which is the voters, can change things. When we asked him how, he said to make sure lawmakers know you're paying attention, that you're interested and following what's happening.

It felt so American to sit in this historic town and talk about important things. I wasn't sure what I would be when I grew up, but I really hoped I could do something that could make a difference. I wondered exactly how hard it would be to change things so they made sense. If my dad's reactions were an indication, I guessed it wouldn't be easy.

Chapter Ten

Sunday night went by quickly and, once again, I was staring at Monday morning. It seemed like every time I turned around, it was Monday morning. I probably should have stopped turning around.

Surprisingly, the week moved along quickly. Between school, the greenhouse, the senior citizens, and New Jersey, our hands were full. Plus, T-Bone and Wanda were busy keeping their promise of regularly meeting with students. I sat in on most of their meetings, and they really were a good idea. Not only did T-Bone and Wanda get feedback and ideas from the people they represented, they also got to explain things. It was actually a great idea.

It wasn't until Wednesday's lunch that we decided to plan our next trip. We were so swamped and as much as we wanted to research the remaining state parks and forests, time was limited.

"Why don't we go to Cheesecake State Park and then Porcupine Park?" asked T-Bone.

"What?" asked Wanda, squinting her eyes as if that would help his answer make sense.

"You know," he replied, "a bunch of kids suggested Cheesecake and Porcupine Parks. We should go there."

"It's Cheesequake and Poricy Park," I corrected.

"Are you sure?" he asked.

"I'm quite sure," I nodded. "But I'll definitely want to know how they got those names."

I had reached a point where I looked at the names of schools, towns, counties, and streets, and wondered who they were named after and why they received that honor. Of course, my street, Dandelion Court, was not named after anyone important or famous, it was named after a flower. And it wasn't even New Jersey's flower, the violet; it was just a flower. If I ever became a developer or city planner, I would name the streets after people who've done something for the greater good, *not flowers*.

And T-Bone was right; we had so many kids with so many suggestions writing us letters. This was a good time to visit some of the places they loved. When we got home, we pulled out the big envelope.

"Here are the ones we pulled out last time," I said as I plopped them on the table.

Wanda started reading them and when we showed her how many came in just that one package, she was very impressed. While Wanda and T-Bone read over the letters, I decided to see if the two sites were near each other. How great it would be, I thought, if we could visit both in one day.

"Hey, good news," I announced as I examined Google Maps on our computer. "These two sites are really close to one another."

"That's nice," said T-Bone.

"More than nice," I continued, "that means we can visit both in one day."

"Oh," said T-Bone, "how about Saturday?"

"I'm free," said Wanda. "I can do the research."

I didn't know where she found the time to do everything else and still get our research done. *I started wondering if she had her own assistant.*

We called my grandfather and agreed to leave at 8 o'clock because we were visiting two parks. I decided to reserve Sunday for sleep.

Saturday morning, I was happy that the weather would cooperate. The meteorologists on the news were even using words like gorgeous, majestic, and magnificent. We piled into the car, my grandfather at the wheel, and headed to Poricy Park in Red Bank. I knew it was near Keansburg, one of my favorite old-school amusement parks.

"Are you ready for some details?" asked Wanda.

"Hit me," said T-Bone.

"Don't tempt me," she said as she shook her head and shuffled her papers. "So, I went on the Poricy Park website, which by the way, I highly recommend. Since 1970, Poricy Park Conservancy has been preserving 250 acres of open space, wildlife and their habitats, prehistoric fossil beds, and the Historic Murray Farmhouse."

"Wow," said T-Bone. "They have prehistoric fossil beds?"

"And an historic farmhouse," she said. "Which means you'll get your nature and history combo today."

"My favorite combo," he said with a smile.

"Poricy Park," she continued reading, "is an exceptional ecological resource whose 250 acres make it one of the largest parks in Monmouth County. Poricy Park is a regional resource, serving residents throughout New Jersey and the Tri-State Area. The park is a center for environmental and cultural education, enhancing the community's enjoyment and appreciation of nature and local history."

"Sounds good," I said. "Do you have more information about the farmhouse you mentioned?"

"I printed this right from their website," she continued. *"The Murray farmhouse and barn at Poricy Park are outstanding examples of middle-class structures from Colonial times. Built in 1770 by Joseph Murray, a stonemason from Ireland, the farmhouse and barn remain on original foundations. Simple plastered walls and brick fireplaces understate the sturdiness and charm of the original five-room house. In the rolling fields setting of the park, a tour through the farmhouse and barn includes few intrusions from the 21st century."*

"That's cool and well-written," said T-Bone. "So many times we tour fancy historic homes; it'll be nice to visit a middle-class home. How long did the Murrays stay there?"

"The property stayed in the possession of the Murray family until 1861," she read. "It was in approximately 1840 when a Murray grandson added to the house. The addition was retained to afford more room for programs. The property was farmed and the farmhouse inhabited until it was purchased in 1973 by Middletown Township."

"Wow," I said, "you mean someone lived in the house until 1973? Pop, you were definitely alive in 1973."

"Thanks for the reminder," he said as he shook his head.

"I wonder why the township bought it," I said.

"I'm just guessing," said my grandfather, "but I'd bet you the last owners wanted to sell, and some developers saw a nice piece of farmland. Where most people see corn stalks, some developers see tract housing and dollar signs."

"What's tract housing?" asked T-Bone. "And that's cool if we're both looking at the same thing and we see something different. Were they wearing special glasses?"

"No, no, no," my grandfather laughed. "It means two people can stand there and look at the same thing and visualize different things. One person looks at a piece of land and sees grass and trees, another person sees a beautiful garden, another sees a park with a playground, and another sees developments full of tract houses."

"Does it only work if they're standing?" T-Bone wondered.

"Yes," my grandfather said, deciding to have a little fun with him. "Yes, if you sit, everyone sees the same thing."

"That's wild," he said, shaking his head, completely unaware that my grandfather was joking with him.

"Anyhow," Wanda tried to get back on topic, "the purchase was made at the encouragement of the Poricy Park Citizens Committee to save the land from development. The 250 acres now known as Poricy Park were acquired by Middletown Township through a series of land purchases from 1970 to 1973. In 1973, no one knew the historic significance of the farmhouse and barn. Use and general repair of the buildings led to research revealing the rich history of the Murrays and their property. The barn was restored in 1978 and the farmhouse in 1981. They're still the property of Middletown Township and maintained by Poricy Park Conservancy."

"Finally, a happy ending!" T-Bone gushed.

"There's also a Colonial Garden," Wanda added. "I read that, in 2007, members of the park tilled a section of land to create a Colonial Garden at the historic Murray Farmstead. Sweet corn, peas, beans, carrots, and more have been harvested during the season. Rebecca Murray would have been pleased with these results!"

"That's awesome," I said. "It reminds me of the Heirloom Garden at the Trent House in Trenton. Remember how cool that was when we saw red and blue potatoes."

"Red and blue skin?" asked Wanda.

"No, the insides of the potatoes were red and blue," I explained. "Lots of vegetables they planted were different colors than we're used to now."

"And they planted specific plants next to each other to keep bugs and animals away," added T-Bone.

"How so?" asked Wanda.

"Well, they were smart enough to know if you put plant A next to plant B, it would keep deer away, and if you put plant C at the corner of your garden it would keep various pests away," T-Bone continued. "They didn't have all of the chemicals we use now."

"Interesting," Wanda mused, "they had no phones, no television, no computers, no internet, and not everyone had books, yet they could grow a healthy garden without the chemicals we use today."

"What's your point?" asked T-Bone.

"My point is, I think they were smarter than us," she said.

"They didn't have cars," T-Bone smirked. "How could they be smarter than us if they didn't have cars?"

"May I?" my grandfather asked Wanda.

"Sure," she said.

"Tommy, having things doesn't make you smart," my grandfather laughed. "In colonial days people were what we called *self-sufficient*. They kept their own animals, grew their own food, made their own clothing, found their own water; they could do for themselves. Look what happened during Hurricane Sandy."

My grandfather was referring to Superstorm Sandy of 2012. This storm did something unprecedented; instead of going out to sea, it made a hard left turn. It caused billions of dollars in damage; more damage than any storm before her. Houses at the shore were ripped off of their foundations and tossed all over towns, the roller coaster in Seaside ended up in the ocean, and many boardwalks were washed away.

"What do you mean?" asked T-Bone.

"We didn't do well without electricity," my grandfather explained. "Once people realized what happened, they didn't know what to do."

"Oh, you mean lighting candles and playing board games instead of video games?" said T-Bone.

"No, no," he insisted, "so many people had long-term power outages. Imagine if those long-term outages were statewide. With no power for refrigerators, food goes bad quickly. Cell phones and computers lose their charges, so communication is interrupted or lost. Gas stations can't pump gas, so even people with generators wouldn't find fuel to run them. Two hundred years ago, they didn't have those things and they were fine; today, it would be a disaster. Maybe we needed to learn colonial skills."

"Wow, I never thought about that," I gasped. "For as smart as we are, I guess we're not too prepared, are we?"

"Well, young people today are smart and have every advantage that previous generations didn't enjoy," he explained. "I don't think your generation or your parents' generation is less intelligent; I think the priorities are more about fun and recreation now."

"Hey, we could be Generation Recreation," said T-Bone, "or Generation Vacation."

"Neither is good," said Wanda, glaring at him. "Don't you realize it makes us look lazy, and we're all not lazy."

Boy, this conversation has taken a weird turn, I thought. T-Bone didn't quite get it at first, but Wanda knew exactly what my grandfather was trying to say. Maybe we should use our devices and technology to learn about things instead of playing video games. Instead of texting all day, maybe we should read e-books. And instead of posting our every thought and action on-line, maybe, if we have that much extra time, we should volunteer somewhere. Of course, I didn't have to worry about those things since I didn't have a phone or any type of social media account.

"In my opinion," said my grandfather, "the ideas you two have implemented at school with the gardens and the senior citizens are what your generation needs. Learning from seniors and learning different skills is excellent."

"Thanks," said Wanda, as we pulled up to Poricy Park.

The park was really nice, and we decided to start by

exploring the outside. I enjoyed it so much; I wanted to join a hiking club. My grandfather pointed out some trees, and Wanda took a bunch of pictures. I was eager to check out the garden and farmhouse.

The farmhouse felt so historic, and I really enjoyed checking out all of the rooms. I grabbed an event calendar and noticed they had school programs and summer camps in addition to their other events. Places like the Historic Murray Farmhouse made me so happy that I lived in one of the original thirteen colonies. T-Bone spoke to everyone there, including several kids. They told us their families brought them to all of the events, and they were awesome. The final thing we learned was that this was part of the Monmouth County Park System and not a state park. Just when I thought I was getting a handle on all of our state parks and forests, I learned there was a whole new category of county parks. With twenty-one counties, I guessed there could be a lot of them."

We said goodbye to everyone we had met and headed north to Cheesequake. I was hoping we'd have enough time to see everything.

"Okay, next stop, Cheesequake," I announced. "What have you got, Wanda?"

"A surprise," she announced.

"Is it a good surprise?" asked T-Bone.

"Doesn't the word surprise usually mean good?" she responded.

"Not if it's like, *surprise, you have a broken arm*," he said.

"*Surprise, you have a broken arm*?" we all asked at the same time. "What kind of doctor would say that?"

"Here's a good rule of thumb," I said, trying to resolve the dumbest disagreement I had ever heard. "If it's good, it's a surprise; if it's bad, it's shocking."

"So this surprise is good?" he confirmed.

"Definitely," Wanda sighed. "I arranged for a special Cheesequake tour guide."

"Really?" I asked. "Like a park police officer?"

"Not exactly," she laughed. "It's Sarah Cassidy."

"Oh, the girl from Lincroft," I said. "How did you arrange that?"

"I had a couple of questions and I called her," said Wanda. "And she was so nice. Her mom offered to bring her over to the park when we got there."

She borrowed my grandfather's phone and called Mrs. Cassidy to let her know that we were almost there. Then she told us all about Sarah and how her grandmother brought her to the park. She was in the fifth grade, although when she started writing her letter to us she was in Ms. Tardio's fourth grade class.

When we pulled in the parking lot, Sarah and her parents, Arielle and Steven, her grandmother, Patricia, her older sister, Julia, and her younger brother, Daniel, were all waiting for us. She seemed so friendly, and she had such colorful language. She said things like: *this park is my cup of tea* and *this place is a real hot spot*. She told us how she loved animals, drawing, and spending time with her family. She was the middle kid in her family, a position T-Bone and I weren't very familiar with. She was a girl scout who loved tennis and had a gerbil named Squeak and a cat named Twinkle. She also loved Cheesequake and couldn't wait to show us around. T-Bone really liked when she said things like *you're in luck*. We were all excited to meet each other.

First, she took us to some hiking trails. She showed us her favorite, and we loved it. I remembered what she had written about fuzzy animals, and I kept my guard up. While it was too cold to swim or have one of her favorite things, a splash fight, we did get to see the beautiful lake. She pointed out what she called the most peaceful, relaxing beach in the world, and I could picture myself on a lounge chair taking the nice relaxing nap she described.

When I asked her what made it so unique and special, she pulled out the state brochure and started reading, "*Cheesequake's uniqueness lies in its geographical location. Not only is it situated in the middle of the urban north and suburban south, it lies in a transitional zone between two different ecosystems. Open fields, saltwater and freshwater marshes, a white cedar swamp, Pine Barrens, and a northeastern hardwood forest are the main attractions of the park."*

"You are definitely prepared," I said with a giant smile. "And I thought it just had a unique name."

"I can also tell you that it's 1,610 acres and offers the following," she continued, "athletic fields, boathouse, campgrounds, boat launch, concession stand, crabbing area, cross-country trails, fishing areas, interpretive center, picnic pavilions, picnic tables, playfields, playground, restrooms, and a swimming area."

"No wonder you love this place," said T-Bone. "How often do you come?"

"I love visiting Cheesequake," she replied. "It's one of my favorite places, but I love all of New Jersey's parks. My family gets to spend time together and explore, plus it's good exercise. One of our first stops is to the nature center where we talk to Jim, the naturalist. He's so smart, so nice, and he can answer everyone's questions about wildlife."

As we continued our hike, she shared some funny stories about rolling down the hills using her vivid language. It was great to meet another kid who appreciated New Jersey as much as we did. Wanda took a few pictures with everyone, and then a stranger took some pictures of all of us. The poor lady almost got away before T-Bone started talking her ear off. A moment later, I recognized her. It was Karen from the Department of Environmental Protection, the woman we met at Ringwood State Park.

"You kids sure get around," she said as she handed the camera to Wanda. "I hope we're paying you well."

"We don't get paid," said T-Bone, "we're still *unofficial*. But even when we become *official*, we won't get paid."

"It's okay," I interrupted, "we don't do it for the money. We do it so kids will know what an awesome state this is."

"Well, I think we're very lucky to have you," she smiled. "But it looks like you've got a few more helpers today."

"This is Sarah Cassidy," I explained. "She wrote us a letter with pictures about Cheesequake. That's why we're here."

"Great selection, Sarah," said Karen. "At DEP, we love to see families enjoying the parks and exploring together." We introduced Karen to Sarah's family and then we all thanked her. Meeting people who protect our environment and natural resources made us appreciate all of their hard work. The state needed so many people to take care of the things most people take for granted. When we said good-bye to Karen, we told her we would see her soon. *I had a feeling we would definitely run into her again.*

Sarah's family was really nice and even invited us to call them if we had any questions or if we were returning to the park. We promised we would do both. Before we left, Sarah told us she had been on our website many times and really loved it. She asked us about the bill and we gave her the bad news: they still hadn't scheduled our bill for a vote yet. She offered to have kids from her school write letters, and T-Bone thought that was a great idea. Wanda handed her an index card with the State House address.

"You just happen to have the State House Address on you?" I asked.

"Absolutely," she said, kind of smugly. "*Don't you?*"

Chapter Eleven

The next morning, my one day to sleep in, my dad came and woke me up very early.

"Are we going to the grocery store?" I asked, too tired to know what day it was.

"No," he laughed.

"Well, what's wrong?" I said as I leaned up and rubbed my eyes.

"Nothing," he smiled. "Today's supposed to be beautiful; sunny, cool, and crisp."

"Great," I said, rolling over, "thanks for the heads-up."

"I'm not giving you the weather report," he continued.

"Are you gonna tell me about the stock market and give me the sports scores next?" I wondered.

"No," he said as he pulled the covers back. "I think we should go for a bike ride. Call your friends, and we can check out another park."

"Huh?" I asked.

"Wake up, kiddo," he said, "there won't be many more days like today. Winter's on its way; let's go."

"Go where?" I asked, thoroughly confused.

"For a bike ride," he shook his head. "Call your friends, jump in the shower, and come downstairs."

As I got out of the shower, I tried to replay the morning in my head. Let's see, I decided I would sleep in and then I remembered my dad waking me up. Next, I was calling T-Bone and Wanda about a bike ride. Nope, still didn't make sense.

I got dressed, grabbed a sweatshirt, and ran down the stairs. Wanda and T-Bone were already waiting. *How did they do that?*

"Where are we going?" I asked my dad.

"Swartswood," Wanda answered. "Luckily, I had printed information about every state park and forest in the event a last-minute, surprise trip came up."

"And surprise means something good," T-Bone confirmed.

"I get that," I nodded. "Isn't Swartswood kind of far?"

"Yes, it is," said Wanda. "It's in Newton."

"Newton?" I said to T-Bone. "We've been to Newton before. We went to Newton on our first Garden State Adventure, remember the fire museum?"

"Of course," he answered, "then we went to Stokes State Forest, High Point State Park, and Lake Marcia."

Before I could figure out what was happening, my dad and my brother, Timmy, walked through the front door. My dad announced that all of the bikes were loaded on the rack and a cooler was filled with drinks and snacks. As we piled into the van, I was still confused.

"Did we discuss this already and I just forgot?" I asked.

"Nope," he said.

"You just woke up early and decided to bring all of us, *including T-Bone*, on a long drive to ride bikes in a state park?" I continued. "That doesn't make sense."

"It's a beautiful day, and I'd like to spend it outside with my boys and their friends," he insisted.

"That's not why," Timmy laughed. "Mom told him that today was cousin Gina's bridal shower."

"So?" I asked. "Mom and the girls have to go to a shower. What does that have to do with us?"

"Because Dad didn't realize the whole family was invited," Timmy giggled. "When Mom warned him that there would be over a hundred people and a forty-five minute video of cousin Gina's life, he told her that he already promised to take us bike riding."

"Oh, so this whole thing is so you don't have to go to a bridal shower?" I asked.

"Absolutely," he said. "Have you ever been to one of those things?"

"No," I shook my head, "*have you?*"

"Yeah, mine," he replied.

"You went to a bridal shower?" I laughed.

"I had to," he explained. "Your mother made me. It was awful. We had 150 people, and I didn't know most of them. The meal took forever, then they played games, then we opened presents. It was just awful."

"I have to tell you, Mr. A.," said T-Bone. "That doesn't sound that bad; I mean, food, games, and gifts. Did you ever think that *maybe it's you*?"

"Kid, you have no idea," my dad insisted. "The games are like cleaning-product bingo and who knows most about the bride. And the gifts; don't get me started on the gifts."

"What could be so bad about gifts?" I wondered. "I think T-Bone's right; *it's just you*."

"Oh yeah," he exclaimed. "Imagine you're the only guy in a room of 150 women. They've all turned their chairs into a half circle to see the unwrapping of the gifts. The table of gifts is endless and each time your fiancée is handed a gift, she very gingerly and very slowly takes off the wrapping paper. Then, she opens the box, ignoring tape and Styrofoam, taking every item out of the box."

"Wow," we all said together, "we had no idea."

"That's not the worst part," he said. "After she took each item out, I had to hold it up while tables of women, each with a combined age of 967, yelled things like *hold it up higher, I can't see it, why isn't he holding it higher?*"

"She opened every box like she does at Christmas?" I asked in horror. "Remember when you bought her a new set of dishes and she took each one out of the box?"

"Do I remember?" he shrieked. "Thanks to your mom's unwrapping policy, I still have nightmares about holidays and showers. The only good thing was that, after our wedding shower, I'd never have to go to another one again. And now, someone in the wedding industry decided that co-ed bridal showers were a good idea."

"*Co-ed?*" asked T-Bone.

"That means men and women are invited," said Wanda. "Although, Mr. A., you forgot the cake. I've been to several showers, and I think they're all about the cake."

"Actually, the cake was good," he conceded, "but no cake is worth sitting through that nightmare. Those are six hours of my life I'll never get back."

"At least you had cake," she said. "One of my cousin's showers had no cake; not even a slice. They wheeled out some kind of cookie cart. I was looking all over for the cake, but no cake. *Who has a shower with no cake?*"

"That's when you know it's a total loss," my dad agreed.

"So, Dad," I continued, "if this whole day of great weather and biking was just to get out of going to a bridal shower, why didn't we just go to the Delaware and Raritan Canal State Park? They have an awesome bike path, and it's a lot closer than Newton."

"Too close," my dad admitted. "When your mom reminded me about the shower last night, I had to think quick. I told her that I promised to take you kids on a bike ride. Before I could think of a place, she told me that she hoped the park was close so I'd be back in time."

"And you just thought of Swartswood?" I asked.

"No," he shook his head. "I told her I couldn't remember the name of the park, that it was on the tip of my tongue. Then I pulled up that Pocket Ranger app on my phone and tried to find a really far park. Swartswood looked good, and far; far enough that I could never be back in time."

I couldn't believe my dad went to so much trouble to avoid a bridal shower. On the bright side, we'd get another park in and also some good exercise.

"Well, I'm glad you picked Swartswood," said Wanda. "Did you know it was New Jersey's first state park?"

"No, not at all," my dad answered. "I just knew it was far and they listed biking."

"Well, it has an interesting story," she said. "If you're done with the bridal shower, I can tell everyone."

"Carry on," he said.

"Okay," she read from a stack of papers. "This park was established in 1914. This park is well known for its fishing and tranquil surroundings. Little Swartswood and Swartswood Lake were formed by glaciers thousands of years ago. They have a 0.6-mile multipurpose trail. People can hike, bike, rollerblade, or skateboard on it."

"The bike trail is only half of a mile?" asked my dad.

"Yeah, it's the Duck Pond multi-use trail," she laughed. "Guess you picked the wrong park for a fake biking story, huh, Mr. A.?"

"Well, I didn't have time to do research," he defended himself. "If I took too long, she would have known I was bluffing. Then, I'd be sitting at a table of ten watching cousin Gina hold up a toaster."

"Let's just make the best of it," she suggested, and returned to her research. "According to Kevin Woyce's book, state-owned parks were a new idea. When the National Conference on State Parks met for the first time in 1921, only nineteen states owned parks. Now, all fifty states have state parks and there are 6,000 of them."

"Good thing we're only reporting on New Jersey's state parks," said T-Bone. "It would take a lot longer to visit all 6,000."

"You think?" I asked in my most sarcastic tone.

"As I was saying," Wanda continued, "in 1914, the state began buying parklands. Swartswood Lake in western Sussex County was named for Anthony Swartwout, who once owned a farm in the area. He was a captain in the New Jersey Frontier Guard and was killed, along with his family, when the French and Indian War spilled into New Jersey from Pennsylvania in 1756."

"Wow, they killed him and his family?" T-Bone repeated. "Poor guy."

"Poor family," said Timmy.

"So, the hilly land around the lake remained sparsely settled well into the twentieth century. Newton, originally called New Town, was founded in 1761 and was a major stop on the Sussex Branch Railroad. Soon the lakeshore town of New Paterson appeared in 1824. By 1852, when the people of New Paterson decided to rename their town after the lake, the lake's name was already spelled Swartswood."

"I think that sounds better," said T-Bone. "Although, if they're changing letters, I'd change the '*w*' to an '*m*' and make it *Smartswood*. Then you've really got something there."

Wanda decided not to address T-Bone's suggestion and moved along. She told us that Swartswood became a summer resort in the late 1800s. Entrepreneurs built hotels near the hills around the lake, and guests launched their boats from George Emmon's picnic grove to go fishing. It sounded like a really cool place. I wondered how Kevin Woyce found all of his information.

"This is interesting," said Wanda, "in 1888, a Newark factory owner named Albert Albright built a lakefront estate. Ten years later, he started charging fishermen a dollar a day to use the lake. Those who refused to pay, he took to court for trespassing. He actually told people that he owned all of the property underneath the water. But wait, it gets better. The resort industry began dying in 1900 when he successfully defended his property rights in the Court of Errors and Appeals."

"Could he do that?" I asked. "And why would he? That's a really rotten move."

"He could and he did," Wanda replied. "That is, until 1906 when Governor Stokes recommended that 108 of New Jersey's freshwater lakes '*be set apart as public parks and correctly preserved for the use of the people of the state.*' Remember, we read that Governor Stokes authorized the Forest Park Reservation Commission to purchase any land surrounding or covered by freshwater lakes or ponds?"

"Oh, that's right," T-Bone remembered. "Whatever happened to Albright?"

"He died in 1906," she said. "His son and daughter sold Swartswood Lake to the state in 1914, and it was the first time the commission bought land solely for use as a park. Two years later, George Emmons donated 12.5 acres of his picnic grove. Since then, the park has grown to 2,472 acres with two lakes for boating and swimming, plus campsites, hiking trails, and picnic tables."

"Did people like this new state park?" I asked.

"It was so immediately popular that it inspired the state to buy and develop other parks," Wanda began her conclusion. "Since 1961, many efforts have been funded by the New Jersey Green Acres bond. They were intended to double the state's publicly owned open space, but so far Green Acres has paid for the purchase, protection, and development of more than 650,000 acres of public land. Other parks or sections have been donated to the state."

"I'm going to donate land one day," said T-Bone, caught up in the moment.

"What are you gonna donate, your backyard?" I laughed.

"When I'm famous," he announced, "I'll donate my house and kids can take field trips to see where I lived."

"And you'll be famous for what?" laughed Wanda.

"I'm gonna be a governor and a senator, a philanthropist, a NJ Hall of Famer, a mayor, and, what else was on my list, Nick?"

"What *wasn't* on your list?" I laughed. "And I have a question: will you still be living there when your house is a museum?"

"Maybe," he shrugged. "Why?"

I could picture a class on a field trip to T-Bone's house. Just as the tour guide enters his bedroom, T-Bone pops up from under the covers. That would definitely *not* be a good idea.

"No reason," I said. "Sounds like a great idea."

We arrived at Swartswood, and it was as nice as Wanda described. The lakes were awesome, and someone told us they held regattas there. I didn't know what that was until my father explained they were boat races. We rode the Duck Pond Trail which meandered around the Duck Pond and decided to hike. We rode back to the van, locked up our bikes, and started walking. When we reached the end of the trail, we considered taking the Spring Lake Trail, a hilly, moderate hike.

Wanda wasn't sure we should attempt a moderate hike, so we walked back across the Duck Pond Trail, once more, to the parking lot to pick up the Bear Claw Trail. It was an easy-to-moderate, slightly-less-than-a-mile hilly path, it was marked in yellow, and it ended back near the parking lot. It was such a nice day and, as long as my dad could hide from a bridal shower, he was happy.

We stopped by Swartswood Lake to check out the lake and its beach. I definitely wanted to come back in the summer. I could picture the beach and water filled with families having fun. Then I could picture this same park with 18th-century families. I wondered if they had known about it. I wondered if they liked to relax and cool off in the water. I wondered if, with all of the work they had to do, they even had time to relax.

I was really happy that Governor Stokes realized it would be more important to reserve freshwater areas for everyone to enjoy, not just those who owned land nearby. It reminded me of Governor Byrne preserving one million acres of Pine Barrens, even when he faced stiff opposition.

I decided to tell Wanda that I'd write this report. I wanted to make sure everyone in New Jersey knew how amazing these parks and forests are and that the best way to protect them is to use them. When I told T-Bone, he suggested we make this *our mission*.

"Mission?" I laughed. "We're not astronauts."

"You don't have to be an astronaut to have a mission," he said. "Our mission should be to save *New Jersey's Great Outdoors.*"

"Okay," I agreed, "but how?"

"The same way you do anything," he explained, "in small steps. First we tell kids about the resources, then we tell them why they're important, then we tell them how they're in danger, and then we tell them how to help."

It always amazed me when he had, out of nowhere, strokes of genius. He was right: small steps and clear explanations. We didn't have to beg or threaten kids to get involved. I knew when they heard the facts, they would do the right thing. My grandfather always said that kids in New Jersey are remarkable. *Now people would see how remarkable.*

Chapter Twelve

When we returned from our Swartswood Park trip, after all of our other park and forest trips, I was inspired. I wasn't just writing a report, I was trying to save our outdoors. The best way to do that was to excite everyone.

It took me a few days to finish my report, but when my masterpiece was completed I was ready to deliver it in person. Before I left for school on Wednesday, I asked my dad if we could go to the state house after school. We had a half day, and I'd be home by lunchtime. Since he was off that day, he agreed.

When T-Bone and I got off of the bus, my dad was waiting on the porch. A moment later, Wanda turned the corner. We left our backpacks in the family room, I grabbed my report, and we were on our way.

"Are you guys hungry?" asked my dad.

When we all said yes at the same time, he asked us if we wanted to go to Checkers for lunch. It was one of my favorite Trenton restaurants and it was very close to some of my favorite Trenton spots: the Old Barracks, the Trent House, the State Museum, and, of course, the State House. It was also across the street from my very favorite mural of the reading of the Declaration of Independence.

We sat at a table surrounded by mostly state and city workers. My grandfather told us that roughly 25% of Trenton's land was used by state buildings, filled with tens of thousands of state workers. It made Trenton very busy during the day. I wondered if we'd see Karen from DEP.

After we ordered our sandwiches, Wanda asked me to read my report out loud. I was happy to. When I finished, the woman at the next table leaned in to speak.

"I'm sorry, I couldn't help overhear you," she said. "My name is Lynn Fleming, and this is Rich Boornazian. We work for the Department of Environmental Protection; I'm the Director of Forestry, he's the Assistant Commissioner, and we are very impressed with what you've written."

"Thank you," I said, "for the compliment and for protecting the environment. We've met several people from DEP at the parks and forests."

"You're welcome," she replied, "but it seems like you're helping us out, too."

"We're the soon-to-be Official Junior Ambassadors of New Jersey," said T-Bone. "Our new mission is to save New Jersey's Great Outdoors."

"That's fantastic," said Rich. "That's an ambitious plan for a few kids. How do you plan to do that?"

"Well, we're actually more than a few kids. We're kind of *a whole state of kids.*"

"Oh, are the rest of them in the bathroom?" he laughed.

"Oh, no, they're not all with us today. You see, we find, visit, and report on great places and a lot of kids and families read our reports," I explained. "We're counting on those thousands of kids to read our reports and spread the word. We're telling them about over-development, litter, air and water pollution, soil contamination, and especially forest fire safety."

"You should meet with Greg McLaughlin," said Rich. "He can tell you all you need to know about forest fires."

"We did," said Wanda. "We met with him at Brendan Byrne State Forest. His information was really useful."

"Wow, you kids are really on the ball," Lynn smiled. "We appreciate you reaching out to so many kids in New Jersey and supporting our message."

"It's our pleasure," said T-Bone.

"Well, on behalf of the Department of Environmental Protection, we thank you," she said as she stood up to leave.

"Keep up the good work," said Rich as he shook our hands.

As they left, we continued discussing our mission and realized the initials would be NJGO for New Jersey's Great Outdoors. When we started speaking about Governor Byrne, the woman at the table on the other side joined our conversation.

"I'm sorry," she said, "did you say you wished you could meet Brendan Byrne?"

"Yes," said T-Bone. "We're New Jersey's soon-to-be Official Junior Ambassadors, and we have a mission to save New Jersey's Great Outdoors. Since he did so much for the state's environment, we wished we could meet him. My friend, Nick, says we'll never be able to meet him and told me to just send him a thank-you card. I'm still planning on meeting him in person one day. I'm not sure how, but I will."

"I might be able to help you," she smiled.

"Do you actually know people who actually know Governor Brendan Byrne?" I asked.

"I do," she said.

"Wow, do you think we could meet him and thank him," asked T-Bone, "you know, in person?"

"I'm pretty sure I could arrange that," she nodded with a smile.

"You mean you can just pick up the phone and call him," I asked.

"Well, let's see, how do you call your dad?" she said.

"No way," gasped T-Bone, "you're related to a former governor? Do you have any idea how cool that is? Did you know he was inducted into the 2011 New Jersey Hall of Fame? And did you know that he preserved the Pine Barrens?"

"Yes, we're related; he's my dad. My name is Nancy Byrne," she laughed. "And yes, it was very cool and quite an honor. And yes, I know he was inducted; I was there."

"Do you know your dad is living the life I want to live?" asked T-Bone. "I want to be a governor, I want to be in the Hall of Fame, and I want to save the environment."

"That's an ambitious list," she smiled. "This is my friend, Linda: she worked in my dad's office when he was governor."

T-bone's jaw dropped. He could not believe he was sitting next to two women who knew Brendan Byrne. When Nancy offered to call her dad and set up an appointment, I thought he would slide right out of his chair. When she said he'd be happy to meet us, he did fall out of his chair.

Once T-Bone regained his composure, we confirmed the details. While I tried to act cooler, I was just as excited as T-Bone. This was big. Meeting a real former governor was huge, especially one that we admired so much. It was all set: Saturday we would meet him at McGloone's Boathouse in West Orange. West Orange was where Thomas Edison had his labs, where Governor Brendan Byrne spent his childhood, and where we would have lunch with a former governor. *This was big.*

When we went to the state house and handed Billy our report, we told him the good news. He was really excited for us. It turned out he knew Brendan Byrne, too. I started thinking maybe we were the only ones who didn't know him. Either way, it didn't matter, because in a few days, we would join the club of people who knew him.

By the time Saturday arrived we were all very nervous. I hoped T-Bone wouldn't be as nervous as he was when we met the Cake Boss, Buddy Valastro. and his whole family.

There was something I had wanted to tell him, but I couldn't remember. When he walked in, I remembered. I was supposed to tell him to dress normal. Too late, I thought. There he was, in all of his glory. He was wearing his suit and his hair was slicked to the side. He was also wearing a great big gold tree pin. I wasn't sure, but it looked like a lady pin.

"Whaddya think?" he asked and spun around.

"I think you might be overdressed," I responded. "And I think that might be a lady pin."

"Overdressed to meet a former governor?" he shrugged. "Impossible. If I had a tuxedo with tails and a top hat, I'd wear that. And the pin is a tree pin to honor the millions of trees he saved. How can it be a lady pin? It's a tree."

"Well, again, I'm still going with you-look-a-little-over-dressed, and where did you get a gold tree pin with a little bird draping a pink ribbon across it?"

"The bird is in honor of the millions of animals he saved, and the pink ribbon is what people tie around old broke trees while waiting for someone to come home," he said.

"You got that pin from your mom's jewelry box, didn't you?" I laughed. "And people *tie a yellow ribbon around an old oak tree.*"

174

"No, I think it's the ribbon used to help old broke trees," he insisted.

"No, I'm pretty sure it's old oak tree," I insisted.

"Old oak tree," my dad confirmed as he opened the door for Wanda.

Clearly, she had asked T-Bone for help deciding what to wear. Knowing nothing about fashion, *even I knew her dress was hideous*. If I didn't know better, I would have thought she borrowed it from Little Bo Peep. She even had ribbons in her hair, knee socks, and shiny black shoes.

"Wow," I said, trying to think of something nice to say. "Look at you."

"Thanks," she said as she stood next to T-Bone. They looked like a prom picture from the 1970s. Actually, with her ribbons, it could have been the 1870s. I wondered what Brendan Byrne would think. Hopefully, we would be sitting before he arrived.

The ride to West Orange was very familiar, and we were too excited to talk. Well, most of us were too excited; T-Bone decided to babble endlessly about nothing and everything. I could only hope he was getting it all out of his system before we arrived at the restaurant.

I wondered how we would find Governor Byrne, but I didn't have to wonder too long. Before we reached the hostess podium, T-Bone was talking.

"We're here to meet with Governor Brendan T. Byrne," he said loudly. Actually, it was very loud.

"The governor is expecting you," she said as she led us to a large table in the back, overlooking the water.

"Nick, look at this place," he gushed. "Can you believe there's water out there?"

"It's called *McGloone's Boathouse*," I whispered. "Were you expecting a desert?"

"Well, there they are," Nancy said as she stood up from her seat. "Dad, these are the kids I told you about: New Jersey's soon-to-be Official Junior Ambassadors who are working to save New Jersey's Great Outdoors. It's their mission."

We were introduced individually, and everyone had a chance to shake Governor Byrne's hand. I was pretty sure T-Bone wouldn't be washing that hand anytime soon. Linda, the other woman we met at Checkers, was sitting next to the governor, and there was a man and two young girls on the other side. Nancy told us that the young girls were her nieces, Alexandra and Scarlett, and the man sitting next to them was Bill, her youngest brother. T-Bone stood there with a plastered-on smile and without moving his lips, whispered, "Nicky, there are five Byrnes and a Linda at this table."

"Calm down," I cautioned, without moving my lips.

Before anyone could decide where to sit, T-Bone had planted himself in between the governor and Bill. While the rest of us jockeyed for position, T-Bone was already buttering a roll and sipping his water.

"So, I've heard good things about you kids," said the governor. "This is good. We need the younger generation to get involved."

"And informed," said T-Bone. "We're telling kids that they have to get informed and then get involved."

"Words to live by," he nodded. "Is there a political office in your future?"

"Actually, Wanda and I are co-presidents of the student council," said T-Bone. "And we all love history. And we're your biggest fans. And we love New Jersey's Great Outdoors. And…"

"And maybe we should let the governor speak," I interrupted.

"Well, you're probably my youngest fans," he laughed.

For a moment, I drifted off, lost in the moment. Governor Byrne was eighty-nine years old and a legend. And we were sitting at his table in a fancy restaurant with his family. I had so many questions for him, but I also had questions for his kids and grandkids.

The waiter came over, and everyone ordered. I was so curious to know what he would order that I didn't even remember what I had ordered. Hmmm, Manhattan clam chowder, I thought. When I snapped out of it, I realized T-Bone ordered everything the governor had ordered.

"So, you'd like to ask me some questions," he said.

"Well, first we need to thank you," I began. "You did an amazing thing by preserving the Pine Barrens."

"Thank you," he nodded. "It was the right thing to do. Of all of the things I did during my two terms as governor, it was my proudest moment."

"Why?" asked T-Bone.

"Because," he began, "while no one opposed the pinelands, no one was prepared to act. I did many things that needed to be done and that others would have done, *but no one was going to do this.*"

"Wow," I said as I shook my head, hanging on his every word. "I read an article that a book inspired you."

"You are correct," he smiled and motioned to Nancy to hand him a book. He placed it in T-Bone's hands. It was the *John McPhee Pine Barrens* book, the book we had read about. He opened it up to page 156 and told us that was the passage that convinced him to act. It was the end of the book, and it basically said that lawmakers will not protect the environment and little by little, the pinelands would shrink until they became extinct.

"But this basically says that it can't be done," said Wanda. "It admits that environmental bills have little interest and support. So how did this inspire you?"

"Because he thought it couldn't be done," he said with a smile. "And I knew no one else would touch it."

"That's pretty courageous," I said. "Were you nervous?"

"Oh, I was always nervous," he nodded. "But I never lost a night's sleep."

"Is that because you were so tired?" asked T-Bone.

"That and the fact that I was doing the right thing," he said. "This was a very tough bill and it infringed upon private property rights, but it was the right thing."

"You didn't have much support from lawmakers, did you?" asked Wanda.

"No, like I said, it was very difficult," he explained. "But I did have support from environmental groups and the League of Women Voters."

Wanda seemed very proud that women were so supportive. He told us that it wasn't a Democratic or Republican issue; no one opposed the pinelands. He said many, many people pretended to support them, but they did nothing.

"Did you always want to be the governor?" asked T-Bone.

"No," he said as he took a sip of his water.

"No?" T-Bone repeated, surprised by the answer.

"No," he continued, "I was an attorney, I worked as counsel for Governor Meyner, I was the Essex County Prosecutor, and a Superior Court Judge. I ran because I thought I could win, and I knew I could do good things."

"You forgot the Hall of Fame," added T-Bone.

"You really are my youngest fans," he said, "except, maybe, for my wonderful grandchildren."

"What would you do if you were governor now?" I asked.

He paused for a moment and, as if he was the president of the former governors' club, told us that he had his two terms and now it's someone else's turn. When we asked him what advice he would have for kids who want to enter politics, he didn't hesitate. He looked us in the eye and said, "Thick skin."

"That goes for the governor's family also," said Bill. "When my dad was first elected, I was five years old. I spent most of my childhood living at Morven, the former official residence for the governor. While it was amazing, some days were difficult. No matter what a governor does, some people won't be happy; it's the nature of the job. But when you're in second grade and people are booing your dad, it gets hard."

"Wow, I never thought of it that way," I said. "I always think of the perks and the cool things. But I guess you probably had a lot of restrictions, huh?"

"Well, the state troopers drove us to school and picked us up," he said with a smile. "They were great. If we were hungry at midnight, they would bring us to get something to eat. If we needed an extra guy to play baseball or football, they would play with us. They really went out of their way to make our lives as normal as possible."

"Was it hard living behind a gate?" I asked.

"As a matter of fact," he smiled, "when we lived there, Morven didn't even have a gate."

"No gate?" I asked. "People could just walk right up?"

"Actually, I remember looking out the window one night and protesters had gathered on the lawn," he began. "The scary part was that they were carrying torches."

"You mean *torches with fire*?" asked T-Bone.

"Yes," he nodded, "*torches with fire*."

"Did your dad call the fire department to turn the hoses on their torches?" T-Bone wondered.

"No," Bill shook his head proudly, "my dad went outside and talked to them."

We were stunned. That was not the ending I expected. I couldn't imagine a politician doing that today. It was brilliant. He just went out and listened to them. Maybe that was what my dad was always talking about: leaders that only connect during campaigns. I couldn't wait to tell him this story.

We also learned that it was Governor Byrne who enacted the New Jersey Income Tax. When we asked him why he was so proud, he explained that it was necessary. He told us many people wanted a flat tax, where everyone paid the same amount. He didn't feel it was fair to ask lower income citizens to pay the same as wealthy citizens. He favored a sliding scale; the amount you paid was based upon your income.

We asked Alexandra, who was twelve years old, and Scarlett, who was eight years old, lots of questions, and it was clear they were really proud of their grandfather and his legacy. While they both played softball, were excellent swimmers, and rode horses, neither mentioned a future run for political office. When we told them about our report on the Brendan T. Byrne State Forest, they were excited. They told us they followed our reports and they couldn't wait to read it. While T-Bone focused on politics, something Bill said really grabbed my attention. He told us his dad was good friends with the former Yankees owner, George Steinbrenner, and that his family spent many games in the owner's box. He actually watched baseball games with legends like Joe DiMaggio, Mickey Mantle, and Yogi Berra. I was completely mesmerized by his stories.

"Do you have a charity for the Pinelands?" I asked.

"Actually," said Nancy, "there is the Brendan T. Byrne Foundation which supports many causes, including the work of the Pinelands Preservation Alliance."

"Wow, how many things are named after you?" said T-Bone.

"Don't forget the arena," Bill reminded us, "the arena at the Meadowlands was once the Brendan Byrne Arena."

I couldn't believe we were sitting here with five Byrnes and a Linda. Arenas, state forests, foundations; it was amazing. Despite all of that, the governor told us that he was honored that we were sharing his legacy with a new generation. I was so excited; I didn't notice T-Bone glaring at me. Once again, he was trying to send me a message with his bulging, wild eyes. His eyes were darting from his plate to the governor and back. His smile went beyond ear-to-ear, and I had no idea what he was trying to tell me. Then, I saw it: the story T-Bone would retell for the rest of his life. The governor quietly leaned in and took a French fry from T-Bone's plate. He couldn't have been prouder. *How many kids could say that? He would tell his grandkids this story!*

When the waiter came to clear the table, T-Bone asked to have his fries wrapped. Then, worried the waiter might throw them away, he requested a container to be brought to the table. Everyone stopped talking and looked at T-Bone. No one could understand why he was wrapping his fries, let alone afraid to let them out of his sight. I was the only one who knew the lengths he would go to in order to protect this souvenir.

184

While coffee and dessert were served, we listened to awesome stories from Linda and her days as a secretary in the governor's office. Nancy and Bill shared more stories about being children of a governor, and Alexandra and Scarlett told us their experiences. The thing that stood out the most was how normal they were. For most people, normal wouldn't exactly be a compliment, but for a family that had experienced such notoriety and exposure, it was probably the highest compliment. They were down-to-earth, approachable, and easy to speak to.

Governor Byrne's determination to protect the Pine Barrens, in the face of opposition, was a remarkable example. He told us he was proud of what we were doing and was happy to help us. It was the most memorable lunch ever. He was so popular that several people approached the table to simply say, "Hello, Governor." When lunch sadly came to an end, we all shook hands and T-Bone clutched his fries like a football.

Just as we were about to open the twenty-foot front doors, a gentleman approached. "Governor, Governor," he said as he stood face-to-face with him. "My name is Mike Copeland, and I'm a New Jersey State Trooper. I drove you to the dedication of the Brendan Byrne State Forest and I just wanted to say hello, sir."

"Yes, yes, Mike, how are you?" the governor said with a smile.

"I'm doing well, sir," he replied and continued to tell him how happy he was to see him again.

They spoke for a few moments and then Mike headed back inside. Before we lost sight of him, T-Bone was right behind him.

"Excuse me, Mr. Officer Copeland," said T-Bone. "Did you drive the governor to the dedication of his forest?"

"Yes, sir," he confirmed. "It was an amazing day. All of the bells and whistles you would expect and all of the fanfare he deserved."

"You sound like a fan," I noticed.

"He's a great man," Officer Copeland said. "He did something no one else would have done. The Pine Barrens would have become a giant city, and New Jersey would have lost an extremely valuable resource forever."

"How did you get picked to drive him?" asked T-Bone. "Did you win *rock-paper-scissors?*"

"No," he laughed. "I was part of the Executive Protection Unit. Our job is to protect the governors and their families. At the time, I was on Governor McGreevy's detail."

"You knew more than one governor?" asked T-Bone.

186

"Yes," he smiled. "It was Governor McGreevey that changed the name of the forest from Lebanon to Brendan T. Byrne. And it was a well-deserved honor; well deserved, indeed."

During the drive home, so many thoughts raced through my head. I was just about to jot down some notes to make sure I didn't forget anything important, but then, I stopped. I put the pen away. I realized it wouldn't be necessary.

You see, in life, there are certain moments that you know you'll never forget. There are moments so big that you realize how big they are before they're over. These are the moments that require no effort to remember and will be as vivid when you're ninety years old as they are the day they occurred. Today, T-Bone, Wanda, and I were lucky enough to have one of those moments; *except our moment lasted through an entire meal.*

The End

About Mission NJGO

Saving
New Jersey's
Great Outdoors

Mission NJGO is Nicky, T-Bone, and Wanda's new mission to save New Jersey's Great Outdoors. While this may sound like an enormous mission, it's actually several mini-missions. These mini-missions can be found in Mission NJGO, a new activity book for students and teachers:

Mini-Mission 1: Knowing Your Great Outdoors
Mini-Mission 2: Why They're So Important
Mini-Mission 3: Identify the Problems
Mini-Mission 4: Preventing the Problems
Mini-Mission 5: Research and Raw Data
Mini-Mission 6: Promoting NJ's Great Outdoors
Mini-Mission 7: Spreading the Word

The activity book is available to teachers, for free. Schools may request hard copies or access the book online by visiting www.nickyfifth.com. Funding for Mission NJGO is made possible by NJ Department of Environmental Protection, State Forestry Services,Forest Fire Service through a grant from the USDA Forest Service as part of the National Fire Plan.

Nicky Fifth's New Jersey Contest

Are You a New Jersey Character?

Submit your favorite New Jersey destination to Nicky Fifth, T-Bone, and Wanda and you could become a character in an upcoming Nicky Fifth book. Write a 3-4 paragraph persuasive essay, selling your idea. Make sure your idea is located in New Jersey and hasn't been included in a previous book in the series. Check the website for a list of places already included.

Entries are judged on creativity, writing style, history, and level of persuasion. Do not list numerous locations; focus on one and make sure it is located in New Jersey. To enter, visit www.nickyfifth.com and be sure you have your parents' permission.

Prizes:

1st Prize - $200.00 Barnes & Noble Gift Card
Digital Video Camera
YOUR idea is used in an upcoming book
YOU become a character in the book

2nd Prize - $100.00 Barnes & Noble Gift Card

3rd Prize - $75.00 Barnes & Noble Gift Card

Nicky Fifth's New Jersey
Contest Winners

1st Place - Sarah Cassidy
Lincroft Elementary School, Lincroft, NJ
Cheesequake State Park

2nd Place - Meira Davidowitz
Ocean Township Elementary School, Ocean Twp., NJ
Smithville, Galloway Township, NJ

3rd Place - Jolene Gianone
Lincroft Elementary School, Lincroft, NJ
Poricy Park, Monmouth County

Welcome to the
Franklin Mason Press
Guest Young Author Section

Here you will find stories from our three newest Guest Young Authors, ages 9-12. From thousands of submissions, these stories were judged and selected by a committee for their creativity, originality, and quality.

We believe that children should have an active role in literature, including publishing and sharing their stories with the world. We hope you will enjoy reading them as much as we did.

If you are 9-12 years old and would like to be a Franklin Mason Press Guest Young Author, read the directions, write your story, and send it in! The first, second, and third place winners receive $50.00, $40.00, and $30.00 respectively; a book, an award, and a celebration to autograph books. Send us a story between 150-350 words, about something strange, funny or unusual. Your story may be fiction or non-fiction. For additional details visit:

www.franklinmasonpress.com
www.nickyfifth.com

1st Place   Isabella Irilli
Roebling ES   Roebling, NJ
When I Run the Zoo

When I grow up, I'll run the zoo.
I'll run the zoo, yes, that's what I'll do.

But I'll make some changes.

All of the lions will be tamed to be nice.
I'll bring back some penguins from the cold winter ice.

All of the polar bears would stay in a pool.
I'll make crystal statues, now that would be cool.

I'll put all of the monkeys, in big fun cages.
I'll bring in some turtles of all different ages.

I'll let all the rabbits run through some logs,
I'll bring in some lizards, to play with the frogs.

I'll bring in an elephant, as big as a house.
I'll bring in a fish, as small as a mouse.

All of the leopards will run around on racetracks.
All of the ducks would quack like maniacs.

All of the peacocks will stay out of cages.
And the people would think that my zoo is outrageous.

2nd Place   Brennan O'Keefe
Lincroft ES   Lincroft, NJ
The Hiking Trip

There were two boys, named Nick and Brennan. Nick was 19 and Brennan was 15. They asked their parents if they could go hiking. Their moms agreed. Nick drove to the Paterson Gimlin Forest in California. They got to the forest and took their tent, cooler and flashlight out of the trunk.

Then they disappeared into the forest. They looked for flat land to set up their tent because the sun was going down. Brennan found flat land and they set up their tent. Nick said, "Let's go hiking before it gets dark."

On the way, they didn't hear or see anything. On the way back, they saw a black, hairy, ten-foot bear - it was BIG FOOT!

They ran back to their tent and they got back safely. They got a picture of it so they could show their parents. They slept fine. They were really scared that morning, so they left. Nick drove them back home. They showed their parents the picture and they screamed.

They said, "You are never going in those woods by yourself, again! We were worried you would get attacked by one of those things!"

3rd Place   Jade Fleckenstein
John Brainerd ES   Mt. Holly, NJ
Flora and her Flower Shop

One rainy day in the flower shop, Flora, the owner was not happy. She was not happy because she had no flowers except for one. It was a Morning Glory.

She could have more, but she ran out of seeds. She looked and looked for more seeds. There were no more seeds.

So she sat there and sat there. The next day, the morning glory died, but left a bunch of new seeds. Flora was so happy! She got to planting right away.

In a month, there were 1,000 flowers in the garden. Flora was so happy that she could sell flowers in her store again. She loved her business.

About the Author

Lisa Funari Willever wanted to be an author since she was in the third grade. She has been a wedding dress seller, a file clerk, a sock counter (*really*), a hostess, waitress, teacher, and author. While she loved teaching in Trenton, New Jersey, becoming an author has been one of the most exciting adventures of her life. She is a full-time mom and a nighttime author who travels all over the world visiting schools. She has been to hundreds of schools in dozens of states, including California, South Dakota, Iowa, South Carolina, Florida, Delaware, Connecticut, New York, Pennsylvania, Ohio, Nevada, Idaho, Utah, Alabama, Louisiana, and even the U.S. Navy base in Sasebo, Japan.

She has written twenty-one books for children and teachers. *A Glove of Their Own* won the 2009 Benjamin Franklin Award. The critically acclaimed *Chumpkin* was selected as a favorite by First Lady Laura Bush and displayed at the White House; *Everybody Moos at Cows* was featured on the *Rosie O'Donnell Show*; and *Garden State Adventure* and *32 Dandelion Court* have been selections on the prestigious New Jersey Battle of the Books list.

Lisa, a graduate of Trenton State College, is married to Todd Willever, a captain in the Trenton Fire Department. They reside in Mansfield, New Jersey with their three children, Jessica, Patrick, and Timothy. If you'd like Lisa to visit your school, go to www.franklinmasonpress.com for more details about her School Author Visits.

How to Use This Passport

Unlike Nicky and T-Bone's previous passport books, this one is different. In this book, the boys, and Wanda, are encouraging families to take advantage of New Jersey's Great Outdoors.

To make it easier for families to complete the passport, this passport does not require you to locate a stamp. This passport requires you to simply fill in the date you have visited each destination.

Your mission is to visit as many, if not all, of the amazing outdoor destinations from this book. Once you have accomplished your mission, you will have a new understanding of what makes *New Jersey's Great Outdoors* so *great*.

Check out the trails, explore the water activities, tour the historic sites, and spend quality time with your family. Then visit www.nickyfifth.com and tell us about your amazing adventures.

Passport to the Great Outdoors

Visit the locations below and use the box to record the date.

Hammonton	Hammonton	Hewitt
Wharton State Forest	Batsto Village	Abraham Hewitt State Forest
Woodland Twp.	Ringwood	Matawan
Brendan T. Byrne State Forest	Ringwood State Park	Cheesequake State Park

Passport to the Garden State

Visit the locations below and use the box to record the date.

Andover	Newton	Stanhope
Allamuchy Mtn. State Park	Swartswood State Park	Waterloo Village
Stanhope	Hackettstown	Numerous towns & counties
Winakung Village	Stephens State Park	Delaware & Raritan Canal S.P.

Passport to the Garden State

Visit the locations below and use the box to record the date.

Sussex	Branchville	Pennsville
High Point State Park	Stokes State Forest	Fort Mott State Park
Red Bank	Galloway	Seaside Park
Poricy Park	Historic Smithville	Island Beach State Park